Retired librarian J. M. Gidman was born in Yorkshire but has resided in Lancashire for a number of years. Her love of reading and history had led her to write two books and several articles on historical subjects. Since finishing her first novel she has written a third non-fiction book. As a member of several local history societies, she has given talks on her subjects of interest. Her first novel was the start of her latest career. This second novel, which is a sequel to *A Question of Identity* carries the story Sally and Ralph Armstrong forward.

She is currently working on a further sequel about the lives of Ralph and Sally.

For all Richards – everywhere

J. M. Gidman

A Question of Authenticity

AUSTIN MACAULEY PUBLISHERS™

LONDON • CAMBRIDGE • NEW YORK • SHARJAH

A CIP catalogue record for this title is available from the British Library.

ISBN 9781398482883 (Paperback)
ISBN 9781398482890 (ePub e-book)

www.austinmacauley.com

First Published 2023
Austin Macauley Publishers Ltd®
1 Canada Square
Canary Wharf
London
E14 5AA

Chapter 1

Ralph Armstrong had been attending meetings all day at the Department of Anglo-Saxon Studies of Jorvik University in York. The start of the new term was just a month away and preparations were well in hand. Meanwhile, his wife, Sally, had been at home looking around for jobs to do. She had already put her own books in apple-pie order and kept looking into Ralph's study to see how he was getting on with his own collection. It was his sanctum and he had said that he wanted to sort it out himself but was not making any progress so far as Sally could see, and she was trying to sit on her hands to prevent herself doing it for him. To take her mind off it, she had given herself the task of sorting the kitchen cupboards out yet again. Sally was not particularly domesticated and had already done it twice but the cupboard layout just did not seem to work for her and so she had had a big think and was having one last try to get it right before Ralph came home.

However, when Ralph came in, he found her on her hands and knees with her head in a cupboard. "Hello, love," he said to her rear as he came into the kitchen. "How are you getting on?"

Sally stood up. Her face was flushed with the exertion and, her dark, normally tidy hair was all over the place. She drew herself up to her full height which was just up to Ralph's shoulder.

"When are you going to get me a job?" she sounded tired and exasperated. "This kitchen is really getting me down."

"Look, darling," replied Ralph, "I keep telling you that you don't need to go out to work. I'm earning enough to pay the mortgage and feed us."

"You're missing the point," said Sally. "I like to get out of the house and meet people. I find I go stir crazy if I am indoors all day. It was OK when we had just moved and you were off to the Jorvik leaving me to sort out all our belongings, which if you remember we never did before we got to York. Just put all my stuff into store and lived out of yours. This is different, now we're here and almost straight, I can concentrate on other things and my mind is seizing up."

"But do you really need a job?"

"Look, sunshine," said Sally. Ralph knew that he was in real trouble; Sally only called people 'sunshine' when she was truly pissed off at them. "I have been an independent woman ever since Adam was a lad and I'm not going to be a kept woman now."

"I didn't know you were that old," said Ralph trying to defuse the situation.

"Don't be funny," replied Sally. "You know what I mean. I love you to bits, Yurrgh I hate that phrase, but I do, but I am also not going to let you walk all over me." And she banged a pan down hard on the working surface.

"Does the pan really need that?" said Ralph.

"No, you idiot, it was a case of the pan or you." And she stomped off upstairs into their bedroom and sat on the bed. She pulled the duvet around her shoulders and sat huddled in a heap.

It was the autumn of 2011 and Sally and Ralph had been settled in the Monkthorpe area of York for two months. They had made the move to York following Ralph's appointment as a lecturer in the Department of Anglo-Saxon Studies at Jorvik University. They had met whilst Ralph was lecturing at the University of West Lancashire in Ormsbury. The move and their new life together had not gone smoothly. They had managed to sell Sally's house in Ormsbury quite quickly because Ralph's replacement at West Lancashire University had been looking for a bijou dwelling in Ormsbury for the weekdays, as she and her husband had a large family home in Cheshire and it saved the difficult commute. Sally and Ralph had then moved into his old family home in Cleckheaton while they looked for somewhere permanent in York. Because Ralph's sister, Ria, had been reluctant to sell her share, Ralph had commuted from home but eventually, his sister had found a purchaser for the house through her decorator husband Alfie as they had realised the impossibility of the situation. And so finally, Ralph and Sally had arrived in York. Their new home was a three-storey townhouse with plenty of room for their combined household goods, their books and with a study for Ralph.

Ralph and Sally had moved from Ralph's two up two down terraced house in Cleckheaton at the beginning of August to a four bed-roomed, three-storey, townhouse in Monkthorpe in York. While they had lived for the year together in Clecky, they had put most of Sally's belongings, from her bijou house in

Ormsbury into storage. This new house meant that they had more room than either of them had known. And for once they could have all their belongings in one place.

The house being on three floors consisted of the ground floor, a garage, and a garden room with a ground floor bathroom and laundry room and stairs going up onto the main living floor. On the middle floor, the kitchen was at the back with an open-plan dining room in the middle, and at the front, the lounge which faced the road but caught the sun in the afternoon.

On the top floor was the master bedroom also at the front with an en-suite bathroom. At the back, there had been the second guest bedroom, which had been turned into two single rooms by a previous owner. In doing this, what had originally been the en-suite for bedroom two, was now the house bathroom with access from the top landing.

The garden room on the ground floor had thus become the main guest bedroom. However, Sally and Ralph had plans for this. It was to become Ralph's study and a library for Sally as there was plenty of space for their books. Sally would have her own bookshelves and space to work when she wanted it but it was to be Ralph's domain. Here there was under-floor heating and so, with no need for a radiator, all the wall space could be shelved. Flat-pack bookshelves had been purchased and assembled with much laughter.

When they had moved in, they knew that the house needed decorating and had, therefore, booked Alfie, Ralph's brother-in-law to do the work. As Alfie had passed the walls as being in good condition, they only needed painting. Alfie had moved in with them and camped for a week and soon the house was completed. They began decorating on the top floor and as each room was finished the carpets were put down and the furniture found a home. Those first weeks in their new home had been quite hectic but once Alfie had finished and gone Sally had begun to feel trapped. She had looked at the curtains they had brought with them, found them wanting in both colour and size and had haunted fabric shops in York looking for replacements. She then set to with her sewing machine was still in the midst of curtain making when September came and with it the meetings that Ralph had to attend.

Ralph was in his element. The problem which he had inherited from his father, and which had beset him for so long, was now finally behind him and he knew who he was and where he had come from. Sally on the other hand was almost a lost soul. She had given up her beloved job in the library at West

Lancashire University and had been unable to get another. Libraries were not recruiting these days, as lots of books were now available via the internet and it appeared that knowledgeable librarians were redundant. *So much for that being a good career move*, she had thought after another futile search whilst based in Cleckheaton.

However, she had managed to find a few temporary jobs in the local area which had tidied her over, and now they were in York she hoped that she could look for something permanent. Ralph, meanwhile, had been lecturing at Jorvik University for a year and was settled but Sally had only been there for two months. Sally's lack of useful employment was turning into a bone of contention because Ralph had now discovered that he liked having Sally at home.

This had led to their first big row in their new home and Sally's departure to the bedroom.

Ralph followed her upstairs and joined her on the bed. "I'm sorry," he said. "I didn't realise just how important it was to you. I know you loved your job at West Lancashire University but you didn't seem to mind when you gave it up to come here with me."

"That was then, and this is now," Sally replied. "I really feel that I could get my teeth into something. In Ormsbury, I had the Family History Society and the Operatic and I have not found my feet here yet. Don't get me wrong; I love living with you but I am more than your appendage. I want my own life too."

Ralph put his arm around her. "OK," he said. "I did ask at the university but there is nothing doing at the moment. Have you been looking for something to do? What do you want to do? I know we looked for library jobs while we were in Cleckheaton but there was nothing not even at Leeds or Bradford universities."

"To be honest, I think I would like something where I can help people. Volunteer perhaps until something permanent comes up. Although I'm not sure there is much of a demand for volunteer librarians."

"What about joining the local family history society, they may need help."

"The Yorkshire one is based in Leeds and I didn't want to travel, they may have a local branch here though."

"I'm sure there must be a York Operatic Society too."

"But that would mean going out in the evenings, and we don't spend enough time together as it is. A city society might be almost professional standard like the Leeds one. I know that the mystery plays are put on here but those kinds of societies might be of much too high a standard for me."

"Look, love, if you find something which appeals to you, go for it," said Ralph holding her close. "I was just enjoying having you to come home to, so as long as you are there some of the time, I'll survive. I have been enjoying the last couple of months and forgot that you were stuck here."

"Right, tomorrow I'll go out to look for something to get my teeth into."

"And I will put my ear to the ground and let you know if I hear of anything at all. In the meantime, I have got a job for you."

"What?" Sally asked.

"Because I love you, and can't bear to see you so unhappy, so as a special treat, I'm going to let you sort out my books."

"You, terror," replied Sally and thumped him on the arm and burst out laughing a sound that he realised he had not heard for several days. "I can't ask for more than that," she said and kissed him. "Now what were we doing before we sparked off? Oh! Now I remember I was sorting out those ruddy cupboards!"

That night Sally woke in the middle of the night and her mind began to race. Ralph laid gently zizzing beside her. This seemed to have happened more often lately which was one reason she had begun to realise that she needed to be more than a housewife. While she did not really mind keeping house and caring for Ralph, she knew that she needed a little bit more. Then she realised why she had woken up. From her work with the West Lancashire Family History Society, she remembered that there was a Family History Society in York. All she had to do was find it. The internet would help. She would look it up in the morning. The decision made she went back to sleep.

Chapter 2

The quarrel actually upset them both. It was not something that they had expected. They had usually got along very equably together so that a major disruption had taken them aback. They had been so busy since their marriage, moving, changing jobs, and setting up house that all their disagreements had been about practical things so a disagreement on such a fundamental subject had rather shaken them.

However, they had made up and Ralph had begun to appreciate that Sally had a point and was determined to renew his efforts to find some worthwhile activity for Sally to undertake. Sally in the meantime had looked into the family history situation in York and discovered that there was a society and she determined to go to the next meeting and find out if there was any way she could help.

During the next couple of days, Sally unpacked and arranged Ralph's books on the shelves in his study and flattened all the cardboard boxes and put them in the garage to await recycling day the book arrangement suited her as it was by author but knowing Ralph he would surely want them differently, and she was patiently waiting for him to complain. But so far, he had not. As a result, she put the second part of her plan to find useful occupation into action, and went for a walk to the local library.

Here she explained her predicament to the librarian and asked if they could help her. She had already joined the library and had used it on several occasions. Despite being already known, her new friends were unable to help her. Library staff members were being given early retirement and even being made redundant and so there were no jobs on offer. However, they could offer her a little light shelf tidying on a voluntary basis and, as this was something that she was eminently suited to doing, she grabbed at the opportunity and arranged to go in twice a week, at her convenience, to help keep the library in apple-pie order. At last, she had something to do which would be useful and outside her new home, which came together with the opportunity to make new friends and contacts.

"Wouldn't it be better if I came in when it was convenient to you?" she asked.

"Well in libraries, we usually spend the first hour or so each day tidying up and shelf straightening but I can assure you, that whenever you can come, we will find you something to do."

Sally, of course knew this but had kept her qualifications to herself for the time being, she did not want to give the impression that she was going to take over, and arranged to go in on Tuesday and Thursday mornings for an hour or so.

Walking back across the park, she stopped to talk to the ducks on the pond. They were clustered around a mother with her child, a boy, in a buggy. Together they were feeding the ducks with bread with the mother giving the boy the bread to hold and the ducks were taking it from his hands. Sally suddenly felt a song coming on and began to hum and sing quietly to herself, *Pigeons, ducks and hens better scurry, When I take you out in the Buggy, When I take you out in the buggy, With the fringe on top*…The mother heard her and looked up.

"Hey," she said, "that's good. Do you do much singing?"

"I used to," replied Sally. "But I was taken very ill about a year ago and my voice went, it's only just coming back."

"It sounds fine to me. Look, I'm in the local community drama group and we are always looking for new talent. My name is Jennifer Smith, known to one and all as Jenny. Would you like to join us?"

"Hello, pleased to meet you. I'm Sally Armstrong." By this time, they were sitting on an adjacent bench while the boy continued to feed the ducks at their feet.

"Well, I've just moved here with my husband," Sally continued, "and I have been looking for things to do. I can't get a job so I've been looking for voluntary work. I used to sing with the operatic society in Ormsbury and was looking for one here."

"There is a big York Operatic Society which is almost professional standard and they give shows in town and the Opera Theatre but we are just a local group of enthusiast amateurs here in Monkthorpe."

"That sounds about my level," said Sally. "I would love to come along and see what you are doing."

"Sometimes we do plays, and concerts and musicals, at the moment we are thinking of doing *Oliver* and trying to get the children involved."

"We did that some years ago but I had to drop out so I would love to get the chance to be in it."

"Our next meeting is on Thursday evening in the Village Hall, do come along. I'll look forward to seeing you there."

Jenny retrieved her son whose name turned out to be Matt and set off home towards the car-park and lunch. Sally set off with her head full of thoughts of new projects in the direction of home which was opposite to the direction Jenny had taken. In just one morning and she had found a job and a hobby and possibly a new friend. Could not be bad.

Later that evening after Ralph cycled home from the university and they were having their evening meal, Sally confessed that she had finally unpacked his books and put them on the shelves in his study. Although she had done this several days before, he had never mentioned it so she thought it was about time he knew what she had been up to.

He went downstairs to his study and she heard him switch on the light. She waited listening for a response which came all too soon.

"Sally, what the devil have you done with my books," he howled, up the stairs.

Gingerly she descended.

"What do you mean? I put them in order so you could easily find them," she said.

"Yes, but what order?"

"Alphabetical by author."

"But I wanted them by subject," it was a cry from the heart.

"You did not tell me that." It was a lame response. "Besides, I don't know which relate to which subject."

"Fair point," he said.

"Let's do it now," suggested Sally. "It won't take long if we work together."

So they sat on the floor of the study going through each book with Ralph saying where he wanted to books with Sally leaning over to put them on the appropriate shelves. As she had said, now that the books were unpacked, it did not take long. Ralph discovered that working with someone else on a task which he, if left to himself would have put off almost indefinitely was much more fun. He also disappeared into the garage and came back with another box which Sally had not seen before. Inside, it were all Ralph's Wainwrights and Birketts which were hangover from his rock-climbing days, and which he for some reason he had wanted to keep from Sally. They were part of his past.

Among the books was one that had belonged to Ralph's grandmother. "Have you ever read this?" he asked.

"Yes, when I had flu years ago, Mum had a copy. I think it belonged to Grandma."

"Well, what about this for a project? Who was Robin of Redesdale? He's in this," he said as he waived his grandmother's precious copy of Lord Lytton's *Last of the Barons* towards Sally. "He was a Yorkshire man, you know?"

"So he was. Goodness you do like finding me obscure things to look into."

"Well, I know your interest in Richard III and Robin of Redesdale comes into that story so why not have a go at looking for him? It could be interesting for you."

"Of course, the main mystery about Richard III is 'Did he murder the Princes in the Tower?' I think that's a bit beyond me. But if I am going to start researching Robin of Redesdale, I shall have to go to the archives as well as doing lots of reading. Are you prepared for me to disappear into books?" asked Sally.

"I shall do my best to manage. Why don't you read this again for now and see what you think?"

Sally put the book on one side and they continued sorting Ralph's books.

When they had finished, Ralph gave Sally a big hug and said, "Thanks, love. It would have taken me ages."

"I know," said Sally. "Someone had to do something, so I made a start."

"Are you trying to manipulate me?" he asked.

"Wouldn't you like to know," was the reply. Starting out in their new home together seemed as though it was going to be an adventure.

Chapter 3

About a week later, Ralph came home to find Sally banging pots and pans in the kitchen, the sound of which rather alarmed him but then he realised that Sally was also singing. Then he realised that the banging was in time to the song. As he climbed the stairs from the ground floor, it struck him that he had not heard Sally singing for a long time. What she was singing, however, startled him even more. "Sisters, sisters, there were never such devoted sisters," carolled Sally.

"What on earth is going on?" asked Ralph.

Sally finished the verse, gave him a kiss and said, "I've had a visitor, and you will never guess who."

"Go on," he replied. "Oh no, not Ria?"

"Yes, your sister Ria, and guess what? She has forgiven me for marrying you. And I have forgiven her for all those things she said about me all that time ago."

"You mean when she called you a bimbo?"

"That's right. She has decided that I'm not one after all."

"But how did she come to visit?"

"I invited her the last time I saw her in Clecky just before we moved. I just said 'Come any time and you'll be welcome.' Today she just turned up on the doorstep. I must admit I was a bit astounded when I saw who it was and also a bit apprehensive but she wanted to have a snoop around so I let her. It turned out that Alfie had told her all about our new house and she was dying to see it. Apparently, he was very impressed with what we were trying to do with it. Anyway, when I had showed her around, she said, 'I didn't think you could do it.' I was a bit flabbergasted 'cos I didn't know what she was getting at, and then she said, 'Make room for Ralph.' Having been told by you that I wasn't after your money, she thought that I was going to have you under my thumb and push you out into the side lines. Some very funny ideas your sister has. It must come from her being the eldest and a bit bossy."

"But you're the eldest in your family," replied Ralph. "And, of course, you are just as bossy."

"Watch it buster. What me bossy? Anyway, Ria seemed to be impressed with what we had done with this blank canvas and the fact that you had your own study while I had to make do with a corner of the dining room. Also, she found copies of the book I wrote about your family and she was quite impressed with that. Maybe I should have kept it hidden, as I knew that she disapproved, which is why I never put them out when we lived in Cleckheaton. Anyway, the secret is out now."

While they were having their evening meal, Ralph went back to the subject. "What else did you talk about?"

"You don't mean that you are interested in womanly gossip, are you?"

"Well, no, not really but knowing Ria, she was bound to say something that might cause problems."

"Actually, the only other thing we talked about was you. She was rather interested to know how you made out as a husband."

"What did you reply?"

"You mean did I tell her the truth or a convincing lie?"

"Mmm."

"Well, I started out with the convincing lie but she saw through that. Actually, she was worried about me. She thought that you might be causing me problems. Apparently, your mother was very concerned about you when you were a child as you kept going off by yourself, and the police kept bringing you home. You were never in any trouble but Mum thought you would be if you kept it up. Anyway, after you went to Leeds University, she thought that you couldn't look after yourself and the long-haired period while you were there, gave her endless worry. You never brought girlfriends home and she was worried about what kind of girls you were getting mixed up with. So, Ria got the worries from her and kept them up after she died. Anyway, I was able to reassure her that, as far as I was concerned, you were not causing me any worries. Also, that you could make a mean shepherd's pie which you had learned while you were at university, and so that up to now you had never starved. I think she went away reassured that we will be OK. I told her to come again anytime."

"You mean I have finally got her off my back. She has been worrying around after me for years, no wonder I never brought girls home. Thanks, love."

17

"I told her not to worry and that you invariably came home without a police escort and that your wandering days are over. That is my hope too. My own mother had similar worries about Les and she shared them occasionally but nothing like that, but I think only Ria would tackle the wife about it. I would never dare speak to Mags about how Les shapes up. Anyway, I think things can only get better!"

That night after they had gone to bed, Ralph began to think over the events of the day. "You know," he said, "I never thought me going on adventures, when I was eight or nine, was having that effect on poor old mum."

"You don't when you are that age," replied Sally snuggling up to him. "You just don't think of the consequences."

"I remember that I always got home but had not realised that the police were involved. I remember them now one was called John and the other Mike. I thought of them as friends. They must have been looking out for me, and brought me home if I strayed too far. Mum must have worried though. The hills were just calling me. Perhaps that's why I never made it to Emley Moor and found the dragon. It all seems so long ago."

"Your mother was bound to worry, let's face it, love, that's what mothers do, boys on the other hand have to do what a boy has to do."

"True," he said and holding Sally tightly they both fell asleep.

Chapter 4

The following Thursday evening, Sally went to the community centre and met the members of the amateur dramatic group. She had initially been a bit apprehensive about going but was determined to go to the first meeting to see what went on and who was there and hoped to meet Jennifer Smith, the lady from the park. Jenny was there and Sally was introduced to so many people, that she had forgotten their names by the following week. However, Sally was asked to audition for a part. As the newbie, and the fact that she had not sung for such a long time, she felt this was beyond her and was grateful to be included in the chorus. The meeting had certainly widened Sally's horizons, and she was glad that she had gone.

By the end of the evening, most of the solo parts had been cast and Sally discovered that Jennifer's husband, Stephen, had been cast as Bill Sykes. Jenny, like Sally, had stayed in the chorus. As she told Sally, "One star in the family is enough." Stephen, despite his casting in such a wicked role, turned out to be a congenial man in his thirties, who it transpired, was a landscape gardener by profession.

"Who's looking after Matt?" Sally asked during the refreshment break.

"We have a babysitting ring in Middle Poppleton," replied Jenny. "So I have a sitter booked for Thursday evenings. It's usually my one night out. That is if Stephen is here as well. Now he has a part he will be rehearsing on Wednesdays until we start putting the whole show together. It works quite well for us."

"Oh, when does that start?" asked Sally.

"Towards Christmas. We learn the music first and the leads learn their lines and some of the staging without the chorus is done on Wednesdays and then suddenly everyone turns up on Thursdays and we're away."

"Sounds hectic."

"Yes, it is. But it all seems to come together. Stuart and Vince seem to get the best out of us."

"They seem a bit terrifying."

"They are in rehearsal but if you meet them outside, they're both pussycats."

"Are you working? I mean are you free during the day? I wonder if we could meet for coffee sometime?" Sally asked.

"No, I'm not working at the moment and I would love to meet for coffee. Most of my friends are working, so I usually take Matt for a walk to break up the day. What about Wednesday?"

"That's great. 10:30 in the Tesco coffee shop?"

"See you then." The break was over and it was back to auditions.

The next Wednesday, Sally met Jenny in Tesco and they enjoyed their break. It turned out that Jenny was a nurse who had taken time out to have Matt and look after him. Soon he would go into the crèche and she would return to work. In the meantime, she was enjoying her freedom.

A couple of weeks later, Sally asked Ralph if he wanted to go to the rehearsal as well.

"Am Dram, is not quite my thing, love," was his reply.

"I know," said Sally, "but I thought it might be an opportunity to meet some other local people, and we might find someone with whom you have something in common."

"Yes, getting to know the neighbours would be a good idea. I know," he said. "They might know somebody who can put me right about the garden."

"Actually, it might be a very good idea to come with me to the community centre because my new friend, Jenny's husband, is a landscape gardener and could put you in the way of getting the garden sorted."

"You didn't tell me that."

"To be honest, I forgot."

"Well, in that case, I will probably come."

"I'll ask Jenny if Stephen is coming this week. He is playing Bill Sykes and the leads don't come every week. I'll let you know when he is going to be there. In the meantime, perhaps we ought to do more things together," said Sally. "You go off to the uni each day and we don't do much in the evening or at weekends."

"What would you like to do?"

"What about going for a drive up to the Dales, or over to the coast and the North York Moors, we haven't been there for ages."

"No, we seem to have spent a most of our time sorting out the house. Does this mean that you think we are almost sorted?"

"You great lummox, It is not up to me to declare that. We should be enjoying life not moving boxes. Besides I need a hobby, or at least to pick up some of my old ones. What about you?"

"Well," said Ralph gingerly, "you know I go to the gym about three times a week, well I have started on the rock wall again."

"Oh, love," said Sally, and hugged him. "I wasn't the one who wanted you to stop in the first place."

"I know but you know me when I say something and get the bit between my teeth and can't let go. I said I was giving it up when we got married, but I could not stay away."

Before they were married, Ralph had met up with a group of university friends each year and they had gone rock climbing to different parts of the country. But on the last occasion, when Ralph had introduced Sally to the group, he had announced that he would not be organising anymore climbing holidays. This had not quite broken the group up but it had altered the dynamic, and now it appeared that rock climbing had played a more significant part in Ralph's life, than he had thought at the time. Sally had not wanted to be the cause of the breakup of the group, it had been solely Ralph's idea, and now he had changed his mind again.

"You mean to tell me that rock climbing has a greater pull than I do," said Sally indignantly.

"You know that's not true," replied Ralph.

"Now I know my place in your hierarchy of importance," she said. "Anyway, are you going to come with me when Stephen comes to rehearsal?"

"Yes, I think I will."

"Thanks, love," said Sally and she kissed him.

Sally's idea of keeping fit in Ormsbury, West Lancashire, had been to walk to the library night and morning and run up and down the stairs while she was there but after leaving and moving to Cleckheaton, she had been a bit of a couch potato. As a result, in York, she had walked as much as she could even just to get the bus. Sometimes she had walked halfway into York and then caught the bus for the rest of the way. However, the idea of going out into the Dales gave her an idea.

"Ralph," she said rather tentatively, "when we go out into the country, would you like to go for long walks to the tops of the mountains? As you know I have no head for heights; I even get dizzy standing on a stool to change a light bulb, so I couldn't climb but I could walk to the top."

"You mean you chose a partner of my vast height to change light bulbs for you?" was his response.

"Don't be daft," replied Sally. "I chose you because I loved you, on the other hand, the fact that you are so tall has come incredibly useful, so subconsciously, it could have played a part. In fact, it was a wholly unlooked for bonus."

"Now I know where I stand in your scheme of things."

"So, are we quits?"

"Yes, I think so." Ralph pondered for a while. "But to go back, your idea of fell-walking that sounds like a good idea. We'll get you some boots and you can break them in before the walking season starts."

"You know it was never my idea to stop you going on climbing holidays with your old mates. If your love of it has come back, why don't you join them again next summer?"

"Wouldn't you mind?" asked Ralph. "I must admit that just at the moment I have been missing it a bit. Perhaps if I go once more, I'll either be able to give it up or carry on `till I get too old."

"No, I won't mind. For heaven's sake, I don't want to stop you doing something you enjoy," said Sally. "Anyway, if we go fell-walking together that will do me, and I can have a week with Lynn while you're climbing somewhere."

"Do you know, love, this marriage lark isn't a bad idea," said Ralph and kissed her. "Thank you."

Chapter 5

Over the next few weeks, Sally fell into a routine of every Tuesday and Thursday mornings, when she would go to the public library and give help wherever and however it was needed. She gradually fell into this new life and began to enjoy herself. Even though she was not being paid, she felt that she was making a contribution to the local community. She had now bought her walking boots and so she wore them as she went to the library taking her work shoes with her. Gradually, the boots began to feel more comfortable and she began to look forward to the following spring.

Ralph had gone with her to the community centre and had made friends with Jenny's husband, Stephen, who turned out to have his own gardening business, and was just what Ralph was looking for. The four of them chatted in the coffee break and it was arranged that Jen, Stephen and Matt would come to Ralph and Sally's and spend a Saturday afternoon with Stephen giving Ralph some ideas for the garden, in a few weeks' time.

In this way, they began to settle into their new life together in York.

Sally was delighted, however, when about halfway through the Autumn Term, Ralph came home and told her that the Gisburn Archives were looking for volunteers and asked if she was still interested.

"How do you mean, am I still interested? Of course, I am. I know it might not lead to anything permanent but it's a step in the right direction. What do I have to do?"

"Fill in this form," said Ralph as he produced it from his pocket.

"You terror!" replied Sally. "Do they want any qualifications?"

"Apparently not, just a willing heart and a steady hand. Actually, I made that last bit up. The form as you will see asks what experience etc you have had but I told Dr Stanley Fisher, the head of the Gisburn Archives over lunch, what you had done to help me. I don't know if he was impressed or not. He doesn't say much but seemed keen for you to apply."

Sally filled out the form and Ralph took it with him the next morning. Two days later, she got a phone call from Dr Fisher's secretary asking her to go for an interview. They agreed a mutually convenient time and Sally breathed a sigh of relief. "Was this the beginning of the next stage of her life?"

She went for her interview on the following Wednesday morning before her usual coffee morning with Jenny. The secretary greeted her warmly and took her through to meet Dr Fisher in his office.

"Mrs Armstrong, delighted to meet you. Your husband sings your praises and I am honoured to meet you," he said with a little bow.

"You've been getting to know Ralph, I see," she replied. "It might be a good idea not to believe everything he tells you until you get to know me better. However, I am very pleased to meet you."

"Yes, I can tell that Ralph likes a joke," he answered as he gestured her to a chair beside a low coffee table. "Let us have an informal discussion. Do you want tea of coffee?"

Sally accepted a cup of tea and as Dr Fisher drank his coffee, the interview began.

"Now then tell me a bit about yourself. You will appreciate that our collections have a unique value and access to them is strictly controlled so we need to know about our staff."

Although a lot of the information had been included on the application form, Sally went through her history, of working as a library assistant at the Brotherton Library at Leeds University, her degree with the Open University, and her library qualifications and her post as an Assistant Librarian at the University of West Lancashire at Ormsbury. She told him of her interest in family history, and how this had led to Ralph's quest for an answer to his family mystery, and her search to find that answer.

"Now I can see why Ralph sings your praises," Dr Fisher said. "Come along and I will show you around the Gisburn Archives."

They began in the public areas where the catalogues and microfilm and microfiche readers were situated and then into the stacks the secure area of the store through the temperature and humidity-controlled doors, and into the heart of the archive.

Rows upon rows of boxes of documents greeted them. Each one was identified by a series of letters and numbers with an occasional word included. Dr Fisher explained the system by which they identified the contents of each box and the need for the airlock system of access. From the storage area, they returned to Dr Fisher's office.

"Now then," he said as he motioned Sally to retake her seat, "what do you think?"

"That was very interesting," she replied. "But if you accept me as a volunteer, would I be working in the main body of the archive?"

"No but I wanted you to see how we organised the collection. I have always found that if you see the big picture, the little ones come into focus, otherwise you are working in a vacuum."

"I can quite see that," said Sally. "I know that there is often a book of best practice for the particular library, the way things are done but if you don't know why they are done that way you can't improve on them. I always made sure that my junior colleagues always knew the reason why we did things when I was a librarian."

"Now we've got that cleared up, I'll explain about the project. The Yorkshire Family History Societies have asked us about the possibility of creating an index of witnesses and executors of wills. As you know, wills are usually catalogued by testator but there is a lot more information in a will than just that name. Wills can contain the names and perhaps relationships of the beneficiaries and also include the signatures of the witnesses to the testator's signature, as well as the name of the executor. The witnesses of course cannot be beneficiaries of the will but the executor can and this kind of information can be invaluable to family historians. Therefore, we are planning a project to carry this out. Obviously, volunteers from the local societies will also be invited to assist in the indexing but if you would like to join them, we should welcome you."

"Thank you very much. I have been looking for something to stretch me since, I came to York. Unfortunately, with the various cut backs in libraries, there does not seem to be any hope of me getting a professional job in the near future, and I did think of getting an archive qualification."

"You won't need one for this project but if you find you like the atmosphere here, it is something to consider. Now, as I say we are in the planning stage, and hope to start early after the Christmas break, probably in January. Will you be available then?"

"Yes. I do voluntary work in our local library on Tuesday and Thursdays but could change them if necessary."

"I think that the proposal at the moment is that Wednesday would be the most convenient for the other volunteers. Does that fit in with your arrangements?"

"Yes. Will I be dealing with original documents?" Sally thought of her meeting with Jenny. Perhaps they could rearrange it.

"I'm, afraid so. Is that a problem?" Sally had to wrest her thought back to the situation in hand.

"No. Would I be working in the storage area or in the open areas?"

"We would bring the boxes out into the meeting room on specific days and you would work through the wills, wearing gloves to maintain the integrity of the documents. How are you at reading old handwriting?"

"I've done a couple of courses at a Keele University Summer School in the past, so I am not entirely a novice," said Sally.

"That's good," replied Dr Fisher as he stood up. "Thank you very much for coming in. I look forward to seeing you again in the New Year." And he ushered her out of the room.

Sally reached the entrance to the building and looked back at it. *Wow,* she thought, *this will certainly give me something to do, and will look good on my CV, if I ever get the chance of a job again. On the other hand,* she mused as she walked towards the Senior Common Room to find Ralph and tell him her news, *I do like being married to Ralph; it's just that I want something for myself.*

As time was getting on, she went to meet Jenny for their Wednesday morning coffee.

Jenny was already in the cafe when Sally arrived.

"Hi Jenny," Sally greeted her. "I'm sorry I'm late. I have just been interviewed in the Gisburn Archive for a voluntary post but they want me on Wednesday mornings. It is possible for us to meet on another day?"

"When will you start?" asked Jenny.

"Sometime in the New Year."

"Well, I was going to ask you the same question because I have decided to go back to work once 'Oliver' is over and Matt will go to the crèche at the hospital, so I would have to cancel our meetings anyway."

"Oh, I'm sorry to hear that, and I shall miss our meetings but this new job is what I have been looking for. So far no one wants to pay me but it is all good experience."

"I'll miss our meetings too. They have helped to break up the week. I can see that you need to get out and about and find your feet in York. When I start back at the hospital, I may be on shift so at the moment, I can't promise a regular time to meet but when I know more, I'll give you a ring and we can sort out something. Stephen and Ralph still have to have their get together don't forget."

"That's true," replied Sally. "These get-togethers have helped me enormously, and there is still 'Oliver' to go. I don't want out friendship to lapse."

"I am so glad that Ralph and Stephen seem to get on so well together at the rehearsal," said Jen. "We are really looking forward to coming to see you on Saturday."

"Yes, I'm looking forward to it too," said Sally. *I hope it goes well,* she thought.

Chapter 6

When Saturday came, it seemed to have come too soon for Sally. This would be her first formal invitation for visitors and she was a bit nervous about the catering. So far, the only visitors they had had in York were Alfie, while they were decorating and he had joined in with the upheaval. When Ria had come, it was unexpected and she had taken pot-luck. But now they had invited guests. Sally was nervous.

Promptly at 2:30 on Saturday afternoon, the doorbell rang. Ralph and Sally opened it to their guests. Matt was the first one in. He already knew Sally from the coffee mornings and any shyness had long gone. It was now that Ralph realised that a stair-gate for young children would be needed, if only on the odd occasion. He deftly fielded Matt before he could rush up the unguarded stairs and handed him to a relieved Stephen. Stephen had no wish to see his son and heir tumble backward down the staircase.

The first order of business was the look around the house. Jenny was intrigued with the layout, and Stephen said that he had always wanted to see what these houses were like inside. Eventually, they made their way back downstairs and out through the study into the back garden.

Together they looked at the almost square lawn which took up all the space. The previous occupants and just had lawn laid for convenience. Ralph wanted something more colourful and Sally just wants somewhere that she could sit and think in the summer. Stephen, ever on the ball, took out his tape and measured the plot. He also took out his compass and located north and thus, the potentially sunniest spot for a seating area. They then went back inside after rescuing Matt from what he thought was a sand pit but was just a pile of sand.

Upstairs Sally made tea for everyone, a hot chocolate for herself and an orange juice for Matt. Ralph and Stephen sat at the dining table while Sally and Jenny sat in the lounge area. The men put their heads together over what could be done with the plot. Stephen got out a notebook and began making sketches as he talked to Ralph. By the time they had finished, Ralph had a very good idea as to what was possible, and what needed to be done to get there. Meanwhile, Sally and Jenny got to know each other a bit better.

"How did you two meet?" asked Sally.

"My parents have a farm over towards Northallerton near Aldwark and they decided to go in for cottage holidays," began Jen. "There were some unused farm buildings which they wanted to convert. Stephen was just starting out then, and he advertised everywhere, and Mum and Dad invited him to give his ideas on how they could improve the look of the place. They liked his ideas and he came along and did the work himself. He was still there one Friday night when I came home from shift, and we got talking. This was several years ago. We clicked and it went on from there. Because Stephen was just starting out, we couldn't afford to get married straight away but then Mum and Dad decided to give up the farm and bought a house for themselves at Middle Poppleton and then decided to stay so we got the house, and he got me. What about you two?"

"Well, as I have told you. I am a librarian. Temporarily unemployed. I was working at West Lancashire University when Ralph, came to lecture. He needed someone with family history experience to help him with a family mystery, and I was recommended to him. I was able to help him, and we solved the mystery. I wrote a book about it which was published by one of the local firms."

"If you want any mysteries solved, Sally's your 'go too' person," a voice came from across the room. Ralph had heard what was being said.

"In the course of my investigation, we fell in love."

"Aaah, sweet." Ralph was still listening.

"Concentrate on what Stephen's telling you. Stop listening in. You might hear something you might not like," Sally was getting annoyed.

"I do love it when she gets angry," said Ralph.

Sally burst out laughing. "He does it deliberately," she said.

"Stephen's just the same. Men!" commiserated Jenny.

All the time they were talking, Matt was wandering around the room. If he got anywhere near the top of the stairs, one of the adults drew him away. Finally, he exhausted his attempts at getting down stairs and decided to try for upstairs instead. Jenny went and picked him up and brought him over to where she and Sally were sitting.

"I know," said Sally. "We will have to get child-proof gates. All our nieces and nephews are older and we weren't expecting youngsters just yet."

"You're hoping to have a family then?"

"Yes but we haven't decided anything just yet. I know we have been married for over two years but we haven't been settled until now." Sally paused expecting a comment from Ralph but none came. She looked across at him. He was smiling. He had heard; he just wasn't going to say anything.

Sally stood up. "I had better start making the dinner, supper, afternoon tea, whatever you want to call it."

"Do you need some help?" Jen asked.

"Thanks, it's mostly ready. As you can smell, it's Ralph's famous Shepherd's Pie so there's not a lot to do so."

Matt was perusing the books on the bookcase. "Books," he said.

"I'd better keep my eye on him," said Jenny. "I'd hate it if he decided to tear them up. He does that sometimes, and then he eats the pages. I think, that he thinks, that is how you learn."

Over dinner, which was enjoyed by all, including Matt, they had a general discussion about the problems of traffic in York and getting about before going on to more general things. Stephen was very intrigued with Ralph's Anglo-Saxon Studies and wanted to know all about them and the Vikings. All in all, it had been a very satisfactory day all round. Sally need not have worried.

Later, that evening after the guests had gone home, Ralph said, "To be honest, I haven't met many people outside academia, and I should. You can get too isolated in a rarefied atmosphere and not really know what it going on in the world at large. I am also delighted that you would like a family. You do keep my feet on the ground."

Chapter 7

Their first Christmas in York was also the first that Ralph was able to attend any of the faculty's celebrations at the university. This year he took Sally, who felt out of place as she did not know anybody and she had not yet made a contribution that anybody had heard about. She was just a wife. Ralph's colleagues were friendly enough but there was no rapport.

The first Christmas in their new home, on the other hand, was spent at home with Les and Mags and the children, James and Jen, who came up to see them. Les had been given an overseas posting and it would be the last time that they would all be together for a while.

The bedroom arrangement worked quite well. Mags, Les and the children had the top floor to themselves and Sally and Ralph moved into the garden-room/study. The sofa bed they had bought now proved its worth.

Ria and Alfie came over from Cleckheaton on Boxing Day with their two, Wayne and Lisa, and for the first time the house rang with the sound of children's voices. After they had all gone home, Ralph and Sally agreed that as a future family home their new house would be a success. Sally was also grateful that she had managed to cater for so many. Ralph had shown Les the garden where he had been making plans since meeting his new friend, Stephen, at the community centre.

The New Year came and with it the date for the start of Sally's project at the Gisburn and so on a chilly Wednesday morning in January, Sally presented herself at the doors of the Gisburn Archives. She was shown into the meeting room with a computer terminal and a box of wills waiting for her. Susan Hartley showed how it was arranged. Sally was to enter the reference number of the will into the computer on a spreadsheet, the name of the testator, the date year, and the name of the executor, the witnesses, and the names of the beneficiaries. Beside the terminal was a pair of cotton gloves which Sally put on and, while Susan stood by, in case of any problems, she made a start. Once Susan saw that

Sally knew what she was doing, she left her to it and so Sally's first day at the Gisburn Archives began.

One evening, in early February, during the spring term, Ralph came home from the university in a pensive mood. Sally could not get a word out of him until after their evening meal. Then Ralph said, "I am not sure how to tell you this but I have a bad feeling about something."

"Go on," said Sally.

"Well, you know that we have never talked about the past, at least you have never asked me about other girlfriends I had before we met."

"I did not ask because I did not want to know. I mean anybody that you knew before me was in the past and I could not get jealous about that but if there's anybody I should know about now your life might not be worth living."

"That's the problem. Someone from my past has suddenly reappeared. She used to have an agenda which included me and I wanted to warn you in case she still had it. She's called Marushka Hamilton though she is generally called Marsha."

"Surely she knows you are married now."

"That would not stop her. She has a tendency to roll over anyone in the way. You may have seen her on television. She's one of those television historians who give you endless insights into the seventeenth century."

"Oh yes, I seem to remember watching some of one of those. She lost my interest early on. So why are you concerned about me? You'd better tell me all about her."

"We met whilst I was doing my Ph.D. at Oxford. She was doing one herself and we kept bumping into each other, accidentally, at least that's what I thought at the time. We ended up living together for a while but she had very definite ideas about what my career should be. It was just about the time that I decided to find out about Granddad and she did not like that one bit. It got in the way of her plans. I only wanted to spend a little time researching but no, she had had the offer of a magnificent post, which led to her career as a media celebrity, and now she is coming to York as Chancellor of St James's University. There is going to be a reception for her and for some reason, I have been personally invited. Not just as a member of the faculty. I have a really bad feeling about this."

"Why did you break up?"

"She got this offer and wanted me to go with her, and I put my foot down and said no. I wasn't going to spend the rest of my life following her around, and

I was going to solve my mystery first. She was quite rude about my prospects and said some very hurtful things, probably all true, and we parted. She went on to fame and success, whilst I ended up in Ormsbury."

"Do you think she wants to rub your nose in her success? As in 'If you had stayed with me this is what you could have had'. Or do you think that you are so desirable that she wants you back, or that she thinks that you are going to get the hots for her when you meet again?"

"That's what is bothering me. I have been worrying about it ever since I heard."

"Well rest assured, my darling, I am not going to give you up without a fight, that is if you want me to. I will not let her come between us. Let's face it, darling, time has passed and you may not have the same appeal as years ago."

"Thank you for the vote of confidence in my appeal. I still consider myself a catch among men."

"Well, I still fancy you."

"Some people may want a media celebrity in their life, while all I really needed was a…"

"Librarian," finished Sally.

Ralph laughed. "That's why I love you," he said, and added, "You helped me put my family mystery to sleep and for that I will be eternally grateful. However, I am not going to let anything I did in the past change what I have now with you."

"So, you'll go to this reception. When is it by the way?"

"On Friday evening at 7:30. Yes, I'll go. Unfortunately, significant others are not invited. I wonder why? Anyway, I'll put in an appearance and disappear as soon as I can. Oh, love I can't say I am looking forward to it."

On Friday evening, Ralph attended the reception and was rather subdued when he came home. Sally did not want to question him then and so contained her curiosity until the next day. She asked him over breakfast how the evening had gone.

"As a reception, it was fine," he replied, "but after the introductions Marsha cornered me and offered me a job with the media organisation she is now with, saying that it would put Anglo-Saxon studies on the map. I told her that I did not want that kind of a profile; unfortunately, the head of the department heard her and thought it would be a big boost for Jorvik University and the department.

Now, all I have to do is work my way through the labyrinth of faculty politics, and all I wanted was a simple life."

Sally put her arms around Ralph and held him close. "This was your dream job; you said if that still holds then, we shall have to negotiate the politics together."

"Yes, this is still my dream job. I am enjoying it as it is. I know that it will develop but if I am part of the development process that will be great. Together we can go places but not onto television. Let someone else do that."

"OK, then love I am behind you."

Shortly afterwards, Ralph decided that he would need a lawn mower to cut his newly laid lawn, when it was put down, and bought himself a small shed to keep it in. Sally decided that she would play her own part in this and bought some wood paint and spent a happy afternoon painting the planking of the new shed in alternate bands of murrey and blue. In this, she was making her own statement as these are the colours of Richard III. To make an equal claim to the shed, Ralph fastened an Anglo-Saxon horn drinking vessel above the door. He was determined to turn it into a Mead Hall!

Chapter 8

Several weeks after Sally started at the Gisburn, towards the end of February, came the week of the performances of 'Oliver', and so for three nights and one Saturday Matinee, she was very busy. Ralph, Ria, Alfie and the children came to see the opening night. The performances took place at the library theatre in the centre of York so it meant travelling into town for the evening. All agreed it was great fun and Lisa, the daughter, was quite taken with appearing on stage and Ria knew that her daughter had found a new hobby. Although Sally did not have a part and was only in the chorus, and as any show is nothing if the chorus is rubbish, her contribution was valuable and she found it hard work keeping all her activities going. She had not sung since her bout of glandular fever a couple of years earlier, and so this was her first appearance on any stage for some time. Ralph came to the final performance and stayed for the after-show party which had to end at midnight. This time Sally was determined not to drink red wine, and so had taken her own bottle of white but it soon disappeared, and at the end, she was the only one who felt confident to drive home.

"Do you remember the last time we did this?" asked Ralph on the way home.

"Yes" said Sally. "I acted the giddy goat and accused you of being my stage-door Johnny! Then I went to sleep and don't remember anymore until I woke up on the settee covered in a blanket. That was you, wasn't it?"

"That's right. I think that was the night I started to fall in love with you."

"You mean that you fell in love with an idiot."

"No. I realised that there was a lot more to you than just being a librarian."

"You betcha buster! There always was. The trouble is people make judgements about peoples' jobs and can't see past the facade. We are all people with desires, longings and a sense of humour if you only look for them."

"I know that now. What would life have been like if you had agreed to go for a drink in the Leeds University Student Union with me all those years ago?" he mused.

"I don't know. Maybe then was not our time. But now it is. I think this conversation is getting far too serious for such a night as this. Let's have some music." Sally switched on the car radio a coming from the speakers was the Borodin serenade turned into the musical in Kismet as, *And this is my beloved.* "Very appropriate," said Ralph.

Sally parked the car on their drive and followed Ralph into the house. Inside he pulled her into his arms and kissed her with passion and led her upstairs to their bedroom. The tiredness and cares of the day left them as they made love and fell asleep in each other's arms.

When Ralph woke up the next morning, it was quite early and something was bothering him. Sally laid beside him zizzing gently. *Where do we go from here?* he thought. They were married now. They were settled in York. Sally had found quite a lot of activities to occupy her time. He felt that he was doing well at the university but there was something missing. Suddenly, Sally woke up with a start. "Where do we go from here?" she asked. This so startled Ralph that he could think of nothing to say for a moment.

"I was thinking that too," he said.

"It suddenly came to me how long we have been together and all we have been through and now we are here. What happens next?"

"We have never really sat down and discussed having a family," Ralph replied.

"That's true," answered Sally. "We seemed to be enjoying ourselves too much. I thought it would just happen. But I am pushing 35 now and it hasn't. Do you suppose we are thinking the wrong thoughts?"

"I don't know about that but do we want a family?"

"Yes, I think so. I like children. When Lynn went off to teach, I nearly went too but I stayed as a librarian. I don't know what kind of mother I would be."

"I think you would be a great one. I don't know about being a dad though."

"You could teach him all about the Anglo-Saxons and Beowulf."

"You mean it's going to be a boy?"

"Of course, it will be; they are much more fun. Look how I get on with James known as the Sprig. No, if we have a child it's got to be a boy. If it's a girl, she can go back. If we are going to start a family, then we had better begin soon before it is too late."

"This is serious stuff," said Ralph. "But I like the idea. How do we go about it?"

"Don't be daft," replied Sally. "We begin with something like this." She turned to him and gave him one if her long, lingering kisses which definitely indicated what she wanted to happen next.

Chapter 9

It was a couple of weeks later, while Sally was doing her normal weekly stint in the Gisburn Archive, when Dr Fisher came around with a very tall and imposing lady, who was introduced to her as Professor Marushka Hamilton. Sally stood to shake hands and found herself, for once, a little on the short side. She looked up at Marsha and saw a well-dressed and coiffeured lady, with flaming red hair and a rather tight mouth, which seemed to lack the generosity of nature that Sally's more casual appearance gave to her. *So, this is Marsha,* she thought, as she returned the greeting.

"I'm very pleased to make your acquaintance, Mrs Armstrong," said Marsha. "I have heard a lot about you. I hear that you have made a significant contribution to the project."

"I am only here on a voluntary basis," replied Sally. "So I can't think who might have told you that."

"Sally," said Dr Fisher, "I understand you have made considerable inroads into the project while you have been here. I am only sorry that we have no funds to employ you full time."

"That is very kind of you," replied Sally. "I must admit I enjoy it here and look forward to Wednesdays."

"If Sally is such a treasure, I shall have to see if we can find a spot for her at St James's University," said Marsha.

Oh, no, thought Sally, *now I am being head hunted. She's determined to get Ralph one way or another.*

"That is a very kind thought," she said. "I have been looking for permanent work which seems to be thin on the ground at the moment at least in my profession."

"And what is that?" asked Marsha.

"I am a qualified Librarian," said Sally.

"We must have coffee soon to discuss any possibilities I come up with," said Marsha as she moved on to see more of the Archive.

After they had gone, Sally felt a strange emotion, one that she had seldom had in the past and it suddenly came to her, she was jealous. Jealous of what this elegant woman and her Ralph had had in the past. *This is no good,* she thought to herself, *get a grip. That relationship is over, at least I hope so. Oh! dear, this is not going to be easy.*

That evening over dinner, Sally told Ralph about meeting Marsha.

"What happened?" he asked.

"She came for a look around the Gisburn. Now why did she come on a Wednesday? It's as if she was looking for me. Anyway, she played the flatterer and practically offered me a job at St James's. She asked me for coffee later to discuss it. Thank you for forewarning me. I know what I am up against. Have you had anymore contact?"

"No but I am sure I will. Jeremy hasn't mentioned it either. So, I'm not going to say or do anything until I hear anymore."

"Darling, it would be awful if your post is put at risk over this."

"I know but don't worry we will survive. I survived Marsha once, I can do it again."

"I just don't like the idea of someone trying to control us," said Sally. "Maybe I am just being a bit paranoid. Besides I have suddenly discovered that I can be jealous. The thought of you and her. When I did not know her, and it was in the past, I was OK with it, but now I have met her; the green-eyed monster has begun to stir."

"Look, darling, please don't let thoughts like that spoil us. I never had the relationship with Marsha that I have with you. She was always nagging me to do something other than what I was, I suppose she was trying to change me, but in the end, I dug my heels in and left her. Actually, she left me saying that I would never amount to anything. She may have been right at least until I met you. My life with Marsha was one big battle. However, Marsha was never very devious, she did try to manipulate but tended to go straight ahead rather that sideways though she may have changed since I knew her. Let's just see where all this takes us. In the meantime, let us carry on as usual and keep talking!"

By this time, they had finished eating and Ralph got up to clear the plates and put them in the dishwasher. Sally also got up and followed him and put her arms around him and held him close.

"Hey up, old love!" said Ralph. "We will get through this," as he returned her hug.

Ralph had met Marsha when they were both doing their Ph.Ds and had moved in together a while later. It was only after they were living together that Ralph realised that the great sex that he had enjoyed at the beginning was being used to manipulate him into doing what Marsha thought was best for him. By that, she meant what was best for her. She was ambitious, he had known that from the start but what he hadn't realised was, that her partner/husband/consort was to be her equal in every way. If she was going to be a media personality, then he had to be one too, however much he was unsuited to the role, or even if he wanted it. When it finally dawned on him that this was going to be his future if he did not make the break, he left her, which of course was a severe blow to Marsha's vanity and self-image. The whole relationship had rather damaged his view of women, and it wasn't until he met Sally, that he realised not all women are the same. But when, after careful consideration, he realised that independent Sally would not see him as a means to an end but as a person in his own right, that he knew that she was the one for him. Marsha was now the person she had always wanted to be, a media personality, the chancellor of a new university, an author of popular histories, and he feared she had come looking for the consort she had lost. Marsha had come back into his life, and he feared would try to use the memory of their time together to manipulate him back into her world. But he now had his own world and was not going to change. But first he had to reassure Sally that Marsha was no threat to their relationship.

Despite Ralph's supportive words, and her own knowledge of his love for her, Sally could not help the feeling, that was beginning to grip the pit of her stomach, that things were going to get worse before they got better again, and would things ever be the same again?

Chapter 10

The Easter Vacation was coming up and Ralph, with the best intentions in the world, thought that Sally should have a treat but one that she wanted, not one that he thought she wanted. As a result, and so that he did not second guess her, he asked her if there was anything, she would like to do during the vacation period. He was very surprised by her answer.

"We have been married two years now, and to celebrate I would like you," she said, "to tell me about the Anglo-Saxons. However, if that sounds too much like the day job, and as an added celebration what about visiting some Anglo-Saxon sites around Yorkshire, and as we go you can tell me their significance?"

"Wow," he said. "I was not expecting that. For one thing, I thought you knew it all."

"Oh, no," she replied.

"But you read my thesis!"

"Ah!" She laughed. "Being a librarian means that you tend to know a little about a wide range of subjects but not a great deal about anything in depth. As for your thesis, yes, I did read it but I'm sorry, love, it was a bit too technical for me and I found it heavy going. I enjoyed your introduction and your conclusion and, as you were awarded your degree, I knew that you must have proved your point. At that time, I had fallen in love with you but worried in case you were too intellectual for me."

"You give me too much credit. So, what do you want to know?"

"Well, how did Yorkshire become Anglo-Saxon as I thought it had always been Viking until the Norman Conquest. Let's face it, your university Jorvik, is a Viking name. So when did it become Anglo-Saxon?"

"Good question." Ralph could be visibly putting on his thinking cap. He took Sally by the hand and led her across to the settee in the lounge. "To begin at the beginning," he said as they sat down, "the British were here first. Then the Romans came. They left between 400 and 500 BC. Then lowland Britain was invaded by the Angles and the Saxons from Denmark and Saxony who became the English. In the ninth and tenth centuries, the Vikings from Scandinavia invaded and destroyed some of the Anglo-Saxon Kingdoms. The main Anglo-Saxon Kings were Offa, who built Offa's Dyke to keep out the celts, Alfred the Great who tried to defeat the Vikings and control their spread, and finally Athelstan, who conquered them and assimilated them, in about 937. That was at the great Battle of Brunanburh."

"I've heard of that," interrupted Sally. "Isn't that the one that no one knows where it was?"

"That's right," answered Ralph. "Some people think that it was at Bromborough on the Wirral."

"Is that why you wanted to go to Ormsbury so you could investigate?"

"Well, I did go to have a look. If it was there some excavation would have to be done to find the site. It was a great battle and there should be some trace of it somewhere. However, there is a legend that Athelstan laid his dagger on the altar of St John's shrine in Beverley Minster before going off to defeat the enemy. When he returned, he gave the church the right of sanctuary. But if Athelstan was setting off to fight the Battle of Brunanburh from Beverley, why did the battle take place on the Wirral?"

"So, there is some investigating for you to do?" said Sally.

"There sure is. Perhaps that is something you could look into?"

"I don't think so. I don't speak the language. I'm going to leave that one up to you. Carry on with your story. There must be more to come."

"Even after the battle, the Vikings still had strongholds in the North and East. The city of York was the centre of Northumbria which was largely governed by Vikings. The last great one was Eric Bloodaxe who was killed at the battle of Stainmore in 954. After that, England was under one ruler, until Ethelred the Unready (Being unready), managed to lose to the Danish Canute in 1016. Edward the Confessor, a descendent of Alfred the Great, became king in 1042. He had no children so it was a toss-up between Harold Godwinson and William of Normandy. Harold was in place so took the throne, giving the earldom of Northumbria to his brother Tostig. Tostig betrayed him and sided with the Norsemen and invited Harold Hardrada to invade which he did in late 1066 and King Harold had to rush to Stamford Bridge, just the other side of York, to defeat him before marching back to defeat William of Normandy which he famously failed to do."

"Goodness gracious," said Sally. "I really asked for that, didn't I? And is that the short version?"

"I'm afraid so. If you want the long version, we could be here all summer. I haven't even mentioned Wulfstan, Archbishop of York, under Eric. Let's face it, love, that's what my students spend three years getting to grips with. So, what do you think? Shall we go and have a look around and see where it all happened?"

"Yes, love, that sounds great. I could do with getting out and about visiting places I have known from going with Mum and Dad and now with you. Couldn't be better."

Over the next two weeks depending on their commitments and the weather, they made treks into the heart of darkest Yorkshire. On one trip, they went to Kirkdale, near Kirkby Moorside, to see the beautiful sundial above the church porch which commemorates Orm, who restored the church when Tostig was Earl of Northumberland. They continued on to Lastingham, hidden on the North York moors, and the site of the monastery founded by St Cedd when he came down from Lindisfarne in 563 AD. On another day, they went via Stamford Bridge, and Wetwang, home of the 2000-year-old chariot burials. They then continued on to Whitby and the church at Lythe with its Saxon and Viking remains. Overlooking the sea on its headland above Sandsend, the view from Lythe surely had not changed much in nearly a thousand years. For their final outing, they went to the Saxon church at Escomb. Over the border in county Durham near Bishop Auckland, and built between 670 and 690 AD, it is a lasting example of the hard work of the builders. By the time their journeys were over, Sally had begun to appreciate Ralph's work and the love he had for his subject. On the way home along the A1M, they turned off to All Saints' Church at Kirby Hill near Boroughbridge and its Anglo-Saxon remains which are now built into the fabric of the church.

Knowing that it was back to the usual routine, on the journey home from Durham, Sally tuned to Ralph and thanked him for his patience and for telling her all about his interests. She had, over the years told him of hers but until now, he had not reciprocated.

He smiled. "No, love. Thank you for letting me bring you up to date. Besides which, these trips have done me good. Having been out of the loop for so long, until I got this job in York, I hadn't realised that my memory was slipping a bit. I lecture on Anglo-Saxon Literature and I love that but seeing it on the ground again has reinvigorated my interest. If you love your subject, it is easy to teach it. I wouldn't have missed this for the world."

Sally realised that she was beginning to settle in her new home, was making a life for herself. The future was looking rosy.

Chapter 11

Ralph and Sally had just come back from their Yorkshire/Anglo-Saxon/Viking jaunt when Jenny rang and asked them to go over to spend the afternoon with them at Middle Poppleton. When they arrived, they were surprised to find a charming Victorian double-fronted house with landscaped gardens.

"Wow," they said as Jenny opened the front door even before they reached it. "This is amazing."

Stephen followed Jenny outside and Matt came bustling after. He ran to Sally who greeted him warmly. He remembered her from their earlier meetings.

"Come inside," said Jenny. Ralph hung back as Sally went in, and Stephen guided him into the garden.

"This is a surprise," said Ralph.

"Yes, I know," answered Stephen. "I know it's a bit much but I wanted somewhere where I could show prospective clients what I could do, so that they didn't think that I was all pen and paper with nothing on the ground."

"Well, you've certainly done that. Our little patch is nothing compared to this. And you've even got a water feature. How do you cope with that and Matt?"

"Well, I made the garden before we had him, so I've fenced it off and at the moment, he knows that he doesn't go in there. I know he will eventually, and I'm working on a child proof gate. If that fails, I'll drain the pond, and put the fish in a tank somewhere else."

They went into the house to find that Jenny was showing Sally around.

"I love these Victorian double-fronted houses," said Sally. "But when we were looking around, they were so expensive."

"We were lucky, or rather I was," said Jenny. "This is the one my parents' bought to retire to and then didn't, they decided to stay out at Aldwark, so when I became pregnant with Matt, they gave us this house. They had both this and the farm, for a while. Stephen had already done the garden for them so there was only the house to update."

"It's marvellous, thank you for letting me see it. Hey, Ralph," Sally said as the men came in, "I want a house like this."

"Do you?" he said. "Well at least you have given me a target to aim for." He turned to Jenny and added. "Sally always admires other people's houses and sometimes I feel that I am not up to scratch in providing for my family."

"Oh, you," said Sally. "I can like a house without wanting to immediately move in. Besides, we have what we can afford and I'm happy there." She thumped him gently on the arm.

They went into the drawing room and sat looking out at the garden. Jenny went into the kitchen and brought in a tray of tea, coffee and biscuits, and some juice for Matt who sat contentedly at Sally's feet. Matt looked at her and said, "Books."

"That's right," said Sally. "I'm the one with all the books." He ran off and came back with one of his books to show her. Sally sat him on her knee and he showed her his book and told her the story, obviously it was a favourite.

"I was quite surprised at how long it took us to get here," said Sally. "We're quite a long way from Monkthorpe. What made you join the community theatre there?"

"When we first got married, we lived over towards Bishopthorpe, and one of my friends from the hospital had joined, she lives over that way as well, and I got tickets for one of their shows. They seemed to have such a good time that Stephen and I joined and have stuck with it ever since. The journey's not so bad around the ring road."

"What is it you actually do?" Stephen asked Ralph. "You told me that you lectured at Jorvik but not in what."

"Well, I lecture in Anglo-Saxon Literature. Most people find it rather off putting so I don't go around bragging about it," Ralph replied.

"Well, that's interesting," said Stephen, "because I have always been interested in that side of the North of England. When we've got Stamford Bridge just up the road, how it could be any more interesting?"

"You're having me on?" demanded Ralph.

"No way. Look out ancestors come from here. I want to know all about them."

"He's right, you know," butted in Jenny. "He's got a whole library of books in his study. At least that's what he calls it. I call it his drawing office, where he plans people's gardens."

"So, have you done a course at the Jorvik?"

"No. Can I?"

"We do put on extra-mural courses, for a fee of course."

"When are they?"

"Usually in the evenings but anyone can join. You don't have to have any qualifications to come along to learn."

"I shall have to think about that. I never thought it was possible for a man like me."

"Oh, for heaven's sake, there's nothing wrong with you. Come along, you will be welcome. In the meantime, come over to our place and see my Mead Hall."

"The shed," whispered Sally to Jenny.

"You wouldn't teach me some nice Anglo-Saxon or Viking Oaths, would you?" asked Stephen.

"Why?"

"Sometimes when I get annoyed with people, a good oath might come in useful, and if I use Anglo-Saxon expletives, no one will know what I'm saying or how rude I'm being."

"Unless, of course, they have already done the course. Best check first." Ralph laughed.

Stephen took Ralph off to look at his library. Stephen had noticed Ralph's books in the study at Monkthorpe but had not realised that they were part of his work rather than a hobby, which it was for him. Now he had an expert in tow, he was prepared to go to any lengths to get what he wanted. He thought that the Mead Hall was a good idea. He would certainly investigate it.

Sally and Jenny had settled to a discussion about the community centre and the choices for the musical show the next year. Because of Jenny's new work rota in the hospital, they had not met as often as they had before and there was quite a lot of catching up to do. What with that and playing with Matt, the time soon flew by and it was time for them to leave.

On the way home, Sally realised that they were both settling into their new surroundings and were making friends.

Chapter 12

Soon after their Easter excursions, and having nothing on hand to read in bed, Sally had begun reading Ralph's copy of *The Last of the Barons*.

Ralph noticed this renewed interest in 'The Middle Ages' and began to tease Sally.

"You do know, don't you?" he would begin. "That Richard III was a thoroughly bad lot and murdered the Princes in the Tower."

As Sally was usually just dropping off to sleep, when he said this, she immediately woke up and responded with venom, "No, he wasn't and he didn't." The she would see his grin and knew he was teasing but the first time he said it she nearly killed him. He didn't do it often but was always glad she was able to fight her corner.

As a result, this had all led her back to her interest in Richard III and the Yorkshire Rebellion of 1469, and Robin of Redesdale. The next time she was in the Gisburn Archive, she looked at the index to see if there was anything deposited on the subject without any luck.

Ralph had been getting the garden in order and was hopeful that the planting he had done would soon show promise (I.e. that the plants would actually grow).

Now that the Summer Term was under way, Ralph asked Sally how she was getting on with her walking boots.

"Well," she replied, "I have been wearing them quite a lot to walk into York and I am finding them more comfortable since I knitted a pair of thick socks like Mother used to make."

"Your mother used to knit socks!"

"Yes, she was very handy with knitting needles. Unfortunately, nowadays getting wool to knit with is a bit of a problem, however, I looked for her pattern and found it. She used to knit Les socks when he joined the RAF. No trench foot in this family."

"So, you will be ready to go next weekend?"

"Why, what's on?"

"There is festival in Middleham and I thought we could go and perhaps take in a walk on the fells while we're there."

"But surely it will be all booked up."

"It probably is but you see, my love, I was looking ahead. I know you have not mentioned it to me, but if you remember, last year you said that you would have liked to go when it was too late to do anything about it, so this year I got in ahead and booked ages ago as a surprise for you."

"You darling," said Sally and gave him a kiss. "I know I was disappointed last year but I bet there were crowds, and we would not have been able to see anything properly, so I just sat on the thought. Since I've taken up walking, I must admit I have been longing to visit Middleham again."

"Well, we can go next weekend setting off on Friday and getting back Sunday evening and if the weather holds, we can go for a tramp on Sunday."

"We haven't done a long walk together since we had our abortive trek to find your dragon on Emley Moor when we were in Cleckheaton. That will be grand, good even."

"How do you mean our abortive trek? We set off in good time and got to the top of the moor."

"I know but we never saw your dragon, you did not take your sword (Mind you, health and safety would not have approved), and we did not see your two favourite coppers. So, from that point of view it was a disaster. But apart from all that it was a good day."

"Yes, it was. I never thanked you properly for that day. I know I had told you all about it but I never thought that you would go with me. I had almost forgotten my youthful madness. Sorry about the sword though."

"Well, I had your sister to keep reminding me that you are a wandering boy and that I should keep you on a tight rein."

"If this is keeping me on a tight rein, please keep it on."

"Have you seen much of Marsha lately?" Sally asked not really wanting to know the answer.

"No, I haven't and if I do, I will tell you. You know you have nothing to fear. All that is in the past."

"I know, I just wondered," she said. "Thank you, next weekend is going to be a lot of fun."

Chapter 13

The following Friday evening, after Ralph came home, they packed the car with all the kit they would need, and set off for Bainbridge in Wensleydale. Ralph had booked them into the Rose and Crown knowing that, with the date of 1445 over the door, it would appeal to Sally. He had booked them in for two nights for dinner Bed and Breakfast. Their room was spacious with an en-suite bathroom and a four-poster bed. As it was getting late, they went down for dinner which was eaten in the bar. It was very cosy.

The next day they went back to Middleham for the Medieval Festival, and spent a happy day looking at the stalls, even buying books and other souvenirs, and watching the displays of archery and hawking. Sally bumped into some of the people she had meet through the Richard III Society, and was able to catch up on all the gossip. Ralph was intrigued by the feat of arms on display and managed to find an expert, who was willing to let him try his hand at sword fighting suitably dressed. Sally took a photograph. Perhaps at last she had found her 'Perfect gentle knight'.

After an eventful day they returned, in the evening, to Bainbridge and a welcome evening meal. Ralph was delighted with the sparkle which appeared in Sally's eyes now that she was with people who shared her interests. He began to realise what she had given up to marry him and live on the fringes of his interests. Sally had always been supportive of his Anglo-Saxon interests but had known little about them until they had come together. Now she knew more, and he could now talk to her about his interests but he also realised that he had never really shared hers, and this came home to him on that day. He knew that he would have to widen his own interests to include hers, if they were to have a future together.

Over dinner at Bainbridge, they talked over what they had seen and Sally thanked him again for thinking of taking her to the Medieval Festival. That night they made love for the first time in a four-poster bed which made them both laugh delightedly at the whole idea. As Ralph said, "Wilt thou, my lady?" to which Sally replied, "I wilt."

The following morning after breakfast, the weather looking fair and with the ground still dry, they set of along the road to Hawes, and then Ribblehead, and down towards Horton in Ribblesdale, to find the car park at the foot of the path up Pen-y-ghent. This was to be Sally's initiation into fell walking.

They parked the car and unloaded their backpacks, which were filled with water bottles, high energy bars, and Kendal Mint Cake, without which no expedition would be complete. Sally put on her socks and boots, and together they set off up the path. Part of the footpath was on the Pennine Way until a branch to the right, lead towards the mountain top. Just of the path was a pothole famous to cavers, and down into which, Ralph and Sally peered before continuing on their way.

Once on the path to the top, they stopped for a break and a drink, and Ralph said, "I seem to remember a long time ago perhaps somewhere near the dawn of time, that you said that if you had had your dearest wish, you would have liked to do historical research."

"Yes," Sally replied. "I did."

"Why did you never go in for it?"

"I had to earn of living. I had done my Open University degree while I was working as well as later, qualifying as a librarian part-time, so I needed to work to get back on my feet. I did not have any spare cash until after the accident when Mum and Dad died, and by then I was enjoying working in libraries too much, to just go and do another course," said Sally.

"Why don't you do something now? There has been no job available, and while I know that the volunteer work you do is valuable, you could do something for yourself. How have you been getting on with Robin of Redesdale?" asked Ralph.

"Well," Sally replied, "I have found a number of books and articles about him but there is a possibility that he was actually two people. There was a Robin of Holderness and a Robin of Redesdale. Most people think that this was to link him with Robin Hood and was not anybody's real name. There's also a possibility that one of them was a Yorkshireman, Sir John Conyers of Hornby."

"Why haven't you told me this before?" said Ralph.

"You've been so busy, and I did not make a start until after the production of 'Oliver' was over, so it's only in the last few weeks, that I have become serious about it. I was going to tell you about it when term finished."

"Isn't there another major question over what happened to the Princes in the Tower?"

"Well, greater minds than mine have tried that one. All the academics seem to agree that they were murdered, and that Richard III, either killed them himself, or had them put to death."

"What do you think?" asked Ralph.

"I know you are always teasing me about this but you know, there is no evidence that he did murder the Princes," replied Sally. "Ah. However, I must remember that you are an academic, and I would not want to get you into trouble."

"I can always say that my wife is very strong minded, and has her own ideas, and that I have absolutely no influence over her at all." Sally slapped him gently on the back of his hand.

"Yes, you could but I hope that you would say it with your fingers crossed."

He showed that they were. "So, you would have no problem if I tried to find out what happened to the lads?" asked Sally. "From having little to do you when we first came to York, you're finding me plenty to occupy my time."

"Of course, if you wanted to you could sign up for an MA, and get a degree out of all the work."

"That's another thought."

"Look we had better get on. At our next stop, you can tell me all you've found out."

They gathered up their belongings, repacked the haversacks, and put the rubbish in the back pocket, and were ready to start again. The rest had refreshed them as well as giving them something to think about, and as they climbed higher, they occasionally stopped to look at the view. It was getting near mid-day and sun was high in the sky, and the breeze had warmed up, so they stopped again for a lunch break.

When they had settled down, two more walkers, who had trailed them up the path, caught up with them and joined them for a break. Introductions were made and Jim and Stanley, who had come from Burnley were eager to talk. They swopped tales of the Fells they had climbed. Sally, never having climbed one before, kept quiet, hoping that before too long they would continue on their way, and leave her and Ralph to their discussion. However, when the time came to go forward, Jim and Stanley decided to make it a foursome to the top, and conversation, whilst walking was not easy, and as the wind blew the words away, the discussion remained on hold until much later. However, Sally enjoyed the view and the feeling of exhilaration she got from succeeding in doing something that she had never done before. She sat on the top of Pen-y-ghent and looked at Yorkshire below her or as much of it as she could see, and realised that she could do anything. Ralph egged her on, and gave her support but there were worlds out there waiting for her to conquer. She looked at him chatting with Jim and Stanley, and realised that Ralph was also a people person. A teacher, like a librarian, must enjoy meeting people in order to succeed. She wanted the best for him, and she realised that he wanted the best for her. Together, they would succeed at whatever they decided to do.

Chapter 14

It was late afternoon before they finally got back to the car park. Someone once said that coming down was harder than going up, and Sally certainly found it so. Her legs ached, and she felt as though she had climbed Everest without oxygen but looking back to where they/she had been she felt exhilarated inside. Ralph packed up the knapsacks and, put them and the weatherproof jackets and boots, in the back of the car and they sat quietly, getting their breaths back before setting off for home.

"How tired are you?" Sally asked.

"So-so," he replied. "I am rather glad I had taken up climbing again, even though it was only in the gym, my legs aren't too bad. How are yours?"

"I feel as though I have done the Pennine Way in one day," she said. "But if you want me to take a turn driving, I'll be OK."

"Right, we'll set off and see how we get on." They set off towards Skipton. Initially, they were too tired to talk, and Ralph concentrated on his driving. It had been a wonderful day for weather and there was a lot of traffic about. As they drew near to Skipton, Ralph asked, "What about stopping here for a meal?"

"Do you think the Bay Horse is still there?" said Sally.

"That was the pub where we ate when we eloped?"

"That's right. I think it's at the bottom of the bypass." Ralph drove down the bypass and there was the Bay Horse. He pulled into the car park, and they climbed out of the car.

"Such a lot has happened since we first came here," said Sally, as she put her arms around Ralph, and gave him a hug. "Thank you for a wonderful weekend."

"It sure has," replied Ralph as he returned her hug. "Do you regret any of it?"

"No, my love. It has been a bit difficult at times, trying to find a role for myself without a job but I think I am getting there at last." They held hands as they went into the Bay Horse. They found quiet corner and ordered their favourite dishes from the menu. That was one advantage of eating out, while they waited for the food and drinks to arrive, the conversation drifted back to Pen-y-ghent and the discussion about Sally's historical research.

"You know," she said, "I didn't know much about Robin of Redesdale when I started out. As I said, I have found several books which talk about the Yorkshire Rebellions of 1469 and Robin of Redesdale and Robin of Holderness so there may be two of them. But no one seems to know who they actually were. As I said, Sir John Conyers has been suggested for one of them. There is a possibility that the names are nommes-de-guerre! Also, that the Robin bit was a carry-over from the legends and tales of Robin Hood."

"Now you have set me on a path of research I still have a lot to do," she continued. "How are you getting on? Have you published anything lately? You keep it all very quiet."

"Actually, since I came to York, I have been trying to find a subject to enthuse me. The trouble is, such a lot has been written in the academic press that finding something that is a bit different is hard. I know that the department want something from me for 'Northern History' but to be honest, I am struggling a bit. I've got to have a meeting with my head of department to see where to go from here."

"Does that mean you might lose your post if you don't come up with something?"

"Not right away but I will have to come up with a topic soon."

"If I were still in the library, I could look up what has already been written for you to look at. Can you do that at the university? What about looking again at some of the material written during the nineteenth century and see if it needs updating?"

"That's an idea. New material crops up all the time and articles are written but a synthesis might fit the bill. Thanks, love. Now you are giving me ideas." And he kissed her.

"That's my job. Cooking and cleaning are necessary but it is ideas that make the world go around."

By the time they had finished eating, although it was late, they felt rested and ready for the drive back to York, a journey they made without incident. They stopped a couple of times to change driver and it was near midnight when they got home. A quick brew, a shower and bed both were asleep when their heads touched the pillows.

Chapter 15

Over the next few days, Sally got back into her routine. The weekend away had done her good and made her think of other things outside her normal routine. She did a data search on the computer and discovered an interesting article about Robin of Redesdale and found that one of the candidates for his identity was definitely Sir John Conyers of Hornby the Yorkshire one near Bedale. There was another Hornby in Lancashire in the River Lune valley but they were not connected and should not be confused with one another. She had heard of the Conyers family and also knew that there were some papers in the Gisburn Archive which related to them. She would ask about the papers next time she was there.

In the meantime, there was another problem. Ralph who was in the middle of exam marking and grading at the university, was coming home late and very tired. She had hoped that the move to York would have reduced his stress levels because during the last year, when they were still living at Cleckheaton, and contemplating the move, he had found the journey very stressful. But he still seemed worked up about something. She was about to ask him about it, and also pass on the information that she had found out, when he came home in a fraught state. His normal placid demeanour seemed to have left him. He threw his bicycle into the hallway and shouted, "I can't go on like this; something has got to change."

"What on earth is the matter?" Sally asked as she ran downstairs to the ground floor. She found him sitting on the bottom step. She climbed passed him and sat down next to him.

"Bloody office politics," he said. "We had finished the grading, and everybody agreed on the results. They had been audited, and now some bright spark has suggested that my option is no longer required, and 'Please could I teach something else next year?'"

"I thought that Anglo-Saxon Studies was a must for Jorvik University, and you can't have Anglo-Saxon without the literature."

"You're right there, love. I have always understood that Jorvik University began as a college just after 1066 when William the Conqueror harried the north decimating the original inhabitants. The Abbot of St Hilda's Abbey here in York was determined that the original language and culture would survive and so collected all the manuscripts he could. A later benefactor added to the collection, and then in the 1880s, the college became Jorvik University. So, as you say, the Anglo-Saxon connection goes back a hell of a long way."

"So, they can't get rid of you completely?"

"No but they want to drop literature as it is too difficult for the students. I mean how you can do Anglo-Saxon without literature?" he confirmed Sally's opinion.

"When do you have to go back in again?"

"Not until next week."

"That will give you time to calm down," said Sally putting her arms around him. "How did your students do?"

"Three of mine got firsts, which is why I don't know what is going on."

"Have you ever been in this situation before?"

"No. I suppose that could be because I have never had a permanent job before. I have always been on a two or three year contracts so I just did what I was told. Usually, it was something I was interested in so there wasn't a problem. Here I was appointed, or at least I thought I was, on my knowledge of Anglo-Saxon Literature, now they want to do a course in, Old Norse which I know something about but can't get an option ready for months."

"When would you have to submit it?"

"By the autumn, so it can go into the prospectus for next year." Once Ralph had started to rationalise his thoughts, he had calmed down and they went upstairs to eat the evening meal that Sally had prepared. If he was going to stay late at the university, Ralph would normally eat in the senior common room but otherwise, he came home for his evening meal.

"How will all this affect our plans for the summer?" asked Sally. They had been talking about going abroad again. They had not managed a decent holiday since their honeymoon because of all the changes they had been going through but now they were settled they could make plans.

"Do you know, darling, I don't much care, I am taking you away from all this even, if it is only for a week. Actually, I have booked us on the car ferry from Portsmouth to Caen on 22 July and we can go where we will. I intended it as a surprise but I really think I should have discussed it with you first. Anyway, we can still go if you have nothing that we need to stay for."

"That all sounds exciting but could you discuss plans with me sometimes. I might have decided to take you somewhere really off the wall, and you would miss out."

"Sorry, love, sometimes I forget that I am married and that you have your own opinions about things but only when I am not here. When I am at home, I know you are the boss."

"You know that's not true but we are a team and should discuss things. Remember I have always asked you not to take me for granted."

"Of course, you did. I seem to be having a bit of an off day, sorry, love. Did you do anything about Robin of Redesdale?"

"That's all right, just don't do it again. Yes, I found an interesting article all about him or them. There could have been two. The Conyers name came up either Sir John Conyers, or his son John, is suspected of being Robin. Sir John senior, was sheriff of Yorkshire during the period. He died in 1490. The writer seemed to think that the Gisburn has some papers relating to him. I did look in the index without any luck. Perhaps I was using the wrong criteria; I shall have to have another look for them. Thank you for giving me the idea."

Chapter 16

The next time Ralph met Marsha was at a graduation ceremony at the end of the Summer Term. He attended as a member of his department which was honouring his students, and Marsha had been invited as a guest. The academics assembled in their robes before processing into the hall. Marsha greeted him in friendly terms, and he began to think that any animosity between them had disappeared. After the ceremony, when all the students had become graduates, the staff congregated in the senior common room for afternoon tea. Ralph was talking to one of his colleagues when he realised that Marsha was coming towards him. He turned to face whatever was coming.

"Ralph," she said, "how lovely to see you again. You do seem to have made a niche for yourself here in York. I am so glad that you have finally found a position that suits your talents."

"Hello, Chancellor," he replied. "It's good to see you again. Yes, my students are all doing well. We have had several First class degrees this year, and a goodly number of applications, for next year."

It was as if the intervening years had slipped away. Now here Marsha was. A celebrity and chancellor of St James's University, and she did him the courtesy of remembering him. So, he must have done something memorable. At this point, the head of his department saw who Ralph was in conversation with and came across to join in.

"Chancellor," he said. "Thank you again for accepting our invitation to grace us with your presence at our graduation ceremony."

"You are too kind," she replied. "I would not have missed this one for the world."

Ralph could feel his stomach tightening. He now knew what he had only suspected before, Marsha was deliberately pursuing him. The dean continued to keep Marsha occupied by explaining his plans for the forthcoming year, and the idea for incorporating Anglo-Saxon Studies with Archaeology as well as history, to make a more rounded programme of study. Ralph turned away only to find that his arm was held in a vicelike grip. On looking down, he found Marsha's hand, under the sleeve of her robes, holding him tight. She was nodding as the dean continued to bore her with details of his plans. They did not affect St James's University as it did not hold, or even plan courses on subjects before 1500. Finally, he finished his diatribe and left them to find someone else to expound his plans.

"Ralph, I was absolutely delighted to meet you lovely wife, when I was shown around the Gisburn Archives. She seems to be making quite a name for herself there."

"Yes," he answered. "She still hopes to find a full-time job but is making do with voluntary work at the moment."

"What did she do before you met?"

"She is a qualified librarian and a graduate of the Open University," he said proudly.

"Oh, one of those who did not quite make it into a decent university?"

"She may not have been a full-time student but she spent most of her working life in university libraries, and probably knows more about most subjects then academics."

"Does that include the Anglo-Saxons?"

"No because they weren't studied at the universities she worked in." He was beginning to get annoyed.

"So, you don't have much in common then?"

"We have more in common than you would think. Librarians get treated like second-class citizens by academics and looked down upon but those that do the job properly could probably outclass us in most things. I find academics tend to only see their own subjects, whilst librarians see all those that are being studied."

"You mean we are a narrow-minded lot?"

"No, just blinkered at times. I have learnt a lot from her, just I as her knowledge of the Anglo-Saxons has grown since she has known me. I fact, why don't you come for dinner one evening, and find out what kind of person she is? She will probably surprise you." There he had done it. Done the one thing he was never going to do. Invited Marsha to dinner. It's one thing to meet a former girlfriend/lover on a casual basis, and quite another to invite them into your home to meet your new partner. What had he done?

"Oh, that sounds like a splendid idea, would next Thursday evening suit you?"

Ralph thought rapidly. Next Thursday, no he could not remember anything written on the calendar.

"As far as I know, we're free that evening. However, if you give me your phone number, I can ring to let you know if it is inconvenient." Now he was asking for her number, this gets worse.

"You had better give me your address. Shall we say 7 for 7:30." Oh no, Marsha was taking over.

He gave Marsha his address but he could not help feeling that she already knew it as she made no attempt to make a note of it. While he, on the other hand, added her number onto his mobile phone. What was Sally going to say?

Later, when he told Sally what he had done, she appeared to take to prospect of his former lover coming to dinner in her stride. But her stomach sank as she remembered what Ralph had told her about Marsha Hamilton, and began to wonder if Marsha still had designs on Ralph for herself. Was this the point that her marriage was put in jeopardy? Her knowledge of Marsha was based on the TV programmes which she had found rather shallow. The seventeenth century was the period that she had written her dissertation on for her OU degree and therefore knew something about it. She wanted more from a TV programme than a bare outline. The discussion of the lives of the women in the recent series was the best so far. Now Ralph had invited this celebrity to dinner. What would happen? She had weathered worse storms than this but a direct challenge to her marriage was something totally outside her experience. She loved Ralph and would fight to keep him, if he wanted her but if he wanted to go, she wouldn't stop him. She would just have to keep her wits about her and see how the dinner would go.

Sally feared that it would not go well.

Chapter 17

Marsha arrived on time, and her taxi left her with the proviso that it could be called for. After the usual greetings in the downstairs hallway, they went upstairs to the *piano nobile*. They sat around the dining table while Sally finished the preparations for the meal. Wine was drunk and tongues began to loosen. Sally only had the one glass of white wine that she allowed herself. She knew what happened if she had too much alcohol. However, she always provided plenty of alcohol for those who wanted it. Fortunately, Marsha liked the choice of red wine (Ralph had suggested it). Ralph as usual drank his artisan beer. During the meal, Marsha began to quiz both Ralph and Sally about their occupations. "What are you doing now?" she asked Sally.

"Voluntary work," was Sally's reply. "As you know I have been unable to get a library position for which I am qualified, so I am using my expertise and help at the local library several days a week."

"I thought that you were at the Gisburn."

"No, that is only on a voluntary basis. I am helping with a project which will, we hope, benefit the local family historians."

"And you Ralph?" she said turning towards him.

"Oh, I am quite happy lecturing to my students," he said.

"Is that enough for you?" Marsha asked.

"Yes," Ralph replied.

"But surely you must want more than teaching a bunch of uninterested teenagers?" she was being deliberately provocative.

"They're a great bunch," he said. "They are interested and come up with very pertinent questions which keep me on my toes."

"But why not come onto the TV lecture circuit with me and get some street cred?"

"If you remember I tried that once before and was a total disaster."

"I wouldn't say that. You seemed a bit unsure of yourself but you always knew your stuff."

"I still do but I like a live audience instead of a stupid camera to perform to."

"But that's the way to get on."

"Not for me."

"Well, how about you Sally? After the success of your little booklet, you must be thinking of more than voluntary work. Are you working on anymore little projects?" By this time, Marsha was beginning to slur her words. Marsha's tone was very patronising in the extreme. While the book that Sally had written about the 'Murder on the Dock Road' and its aftermath, could be described as little, it had taken a long time to put together, and she hated anybody belittling it. It may not have made a difference in the great scheme of things but the truth had been told and two families' anxieties had been settled.

"I would like to get a proper, paying job," she admitted, her face getting red. "But in the meantime, I am finding out lots of useful information."

"Now that you have found the answer to your little problem, Ralph perhaps you can go on to bigger and better things." Marsha had known of the effect that Ralph's family mystery had had on him and now she referred to it as 'a little problem'. Ralph could feel his hackles rising.

"Well, I did not find the answer to my little problem, as you call it, Sally did. While I am glad that it has been solved, I now find that I am exactly where I want to be."

"But, darling," gushed Marsha, "that was the only thing that was holding you back. I told you time and again to forget it and get a life."

"Yes, Marsha, so you did, and do you know, I realised that the kind of life you wanted for me, was your kind of life. It wasn't mine. Which, if you remember, was why I left in the first place. Just because my little problem has been solved does not mean that I can go back to being your lapdog, trailing on your coat-tails. I have my own life now, here with Sally." Ralph straightened himself in this chair and drew himself to his full 6ft 2in and looked at his most imposing and his most handsome. "If you have come here expecting us to start again you have missed the boat." He got up from the table and began to gather the dishes to take them into the kitchen. Sally got up as well and helped him gather them together. In the kitchen, Ralph helped stack the dishwasher and when he had finished, he turned to Sally put his arms around her and held her close.

"I'm sorry, darling," he said. "If I had known she was going to behave like that, I would never have asked her for dinner. Her social side is bright and charming, and I thought she had grown up and forgotten me."

"You forget, I met her under social conditions too, otherwise I would have stopped you."

"What are you two doing in here?" a voice from the table. "Oh, it's the two love birds. Come on now, surely, you're past all that now? Ralph, darling, I need some more wine." She came into the kitchen and tried to drape herself around Ralph.

"No, Marsha, you have had enough. I think it's time you went home. I am going to ring for the taxi." He tried to wriggle free of her embrace.

"But, darling, aren't you going to take me home like you used to, and leave the little nestling here," she wheedled, it was obvious what she had in mind.

"No, it's going to be a taxi. And if we ever meet again, it will always be in public if this is how you are going to behave in private. I never was your play thing, and in the morning, I hope you will realise why." Ralph's stern reply had a dramatic effect on Marsha, who appeared to crumple and tears began to roll down her face.

"Oh, lord," said Ralph. "I've never seen her like this. What do we do?"

"Put the kettle on and make some black coffee," was Sally's response. "We can't send her back like this."

While the kettle boiled, Marsha kept moaning and muttering, "No one loves me, and no one came up to you. I thought I was alright on my own but then I saw the years rolling by and I was all alone, and I wanted you."

"That's as may be," said Ralph as between them, he and Sally got Marsha back into the lounge, and on to the settee. "But time has gone on and we have both changed."

Sally made some strong black coffee and brought it into the lounge and gave it to Marsha, who wasn't so drunk, that she was unable to hold the mug. She held it in both her hands and sipped the black liquid. "Oh dear," she said, "I've made a fool of myself, haven't I? I sometimes think of all the mistakes I've made, and losing you, Ralph, was the biggest. Anyway, Sally why should you have him? I saw him first."

Sally was taken aback at this but rallied to reply. "Marsha, for a start, Ralph makes up his own mind about things like that, men do you know, they aren't objects we women can rule over. They are human beings too. Besides I saw him long before he even met you."

"What do you mean?"

"He fancied me when he was a student at Leeds University and I was working in the library. In fact, we have a photograph to prove it. So, we have known each other an awful long time."

"Oh, dear, I have made a fool of myself."

"Look," said Sally, "let's pretend that this evening never took place. Go home, sober up, have a good night's sleep, wake up in the morning and it will have all been a dream. I think it would be best if we do not meet anywhere other than in public, where we can be formal and polite, and forget that this ever happened."

"Sounds like a plan," said Ralph, ever the loyal husband. "Sally always has the best ideas."

"I'll try," replied Marsha. "But when the love of your life marries someone else, it's a bit devastating."

"Well, try not to be devastated too much," said Ralph as he picked up the phone to ring for a taxi.

After she had gone, they looked at each other and both said, "I was not expecting that."

Chapter 18

On the morning of 22nd July, Sally and Ralph set of in their car for Portsmouth and the overnight ferry to Caen. Sally knew that they were going to France and had packed accordingly but other than that, did not know their final destination. This was one concession that she allowed Ralph. He had arranged a lovely surprise honeymoon and she hoped that this would be another delightful surprise.

The ferry landed them at about 7 am the next morning on the coast of France and Ralph drove them passed Caen and down to the Norman town of Falaise where William the Conqueror was born. This, for Ralph, was the worse place because it was here that the decimator of the Anglo-Saxon world, which he loved, came from. Conquering England was all very well but driving a flourishing civilisation underground was quite another.

Together they looked around the castle, still magnificent after all the intervening years. They had lunch at a nearby restaurant and then continued south. Eventually, they reached the valley of the Loire and stopped at Tours for the night where Ralph had booked a hotel for a couple of nights.

"Have we reached out final destination?" asked Sally.

"Not quite, we'll get there tomorrow."

"Am I right in thinking, Chinon and possibly Fontevraud?"

"Wait and see."

"Oh, I do hope so, you darling man. You know how I have always had them on my list."

"I know, I took a peek at it when I was trying to find somewhere for us to go."

"I know that you like surprising me but I would like the option finding a place for you to visit too."

"I thought that I would give you a nice surprise as it had been such a difficult year for you. And last year, we didn't get a holiday because we were moving.

So, I thought that I would take you somewhere you wanted to go. Who knows how we will be fixed next year?"

Sally kissed him. Before she had met Ralph, she was the one who always made the holiday arrangements in agreement with her old friend, Lynne. Since living with Ralph, she had given up some of this independence, and so far, he had not let her down. She still liked to be in charge, and now she knew the final destination, she was content.

The next day, they reached the town of Chinon on the river Vienne just south of the Loire Valley. The castle rose magnificently above the town and dominated any view of the town from the south. Together, they walked around the fortifications begun by the Plantagenets and looked at the history of the Castle and the royal apartments built by a later monarch. King John was here as was Richard I and this was the setting for the Christmas meeting of Henry II and his queen immortalised in the play *The Lion in Winter*. Here the Knights Templar, were imprisoned, by King Philip of France in 1311. He tortured them to give up their gold but they preferred to die. Sally and Ralph drank in the whole experience went to the little cafe for a coffee.

"How are you getting on with Robin of Redesdale?" asked Ralph.

This was the first time in a long while that he had asked how she was getting on. His worries over his future at Jorvik University had taken precedence, and she had let him get on without interrupting his deliberations. She had been as supportive as she could and had got on with her own interests until he had the time, or the inclination, to ask about hers. She had kept him posted about what she was doing but had not told him in detail what she had found.

"Well, I think I have done all the right things. I started out by reading lots of books about the Yorkshire Rebellion of 1469 which turned out to be rather more than that. In fact, there appears to have been several disturbances. First there was unrest in Yorkshire about the tythes paid to St Leonard's Hospital in York, and then another in Lincolnshire a little later. Both of them seem to have played into the hands of Warwick the Kingmaker in his dispute with Edward IV. Both were led by characters known as either Robin of Holderness or Robin of Redesdale wherever that is. And of course, Edward IV was imprisoned by Warwick at Middleham Castle and then at Pontefract but that was later in 1470. But who these men were, seems to be a mystery. Robin of Redesdale could have been Sir John Conyers of Hornby Castle in Yorkshire, not to be confused with the one in Lancashire but he was High Sherriff of Yorkshire from 1467–8 so it's a little unlikely that he would have challenged his king. On the other hand, they were all doing it."

"What?"

"Challenging the king. Anyway, I looked him up in the Gisburn collection and found some Conyers' papers which did not refer to the rebellion at all. Your friend Dr Fisher has been awfully helpful finding me documents to look at. However, I might have to go to Hull, actually I will have to go to Hull, to look at what is deposited there. Just before we came away, Dr Fisher told me that they had received some new documents which seem to be from the right period and he will try to have them available to me when we get back."

"Are you enjoying it?"

"Yes, love. It's a bit different from what I am used to, although I did write a dissertation for my OU degree which involved looking at original sources. The handwriting takes a bit of getting used to but so far, all the documents have been in English."

"You seemed to be enjoying yourself doing this research, so I am glad to hear it."

"If I had known that you going to give me a tutorial while we are on holiday, I would have brought my notebooks with me," teased Sally. "Don't you ever give up?"

"I'm sorry if I have been coming on a bit strong. I really must start to relax. No, love, I was not giving you a tutorial, I was just interested as you hadn't said much. So, you think you might have to penetrate the darker reached of Hull? Mm. I shall have to think about that. I can't have you gadding about Yorkshire on your own, who knows what you might get up to."

"OK, buster, that's it. Don't you come the heavy Hubby with me, or you will find out the hard way what you have let yourself in for marrying a Yorkshire woman."

"OK, I'll give you Hull. Now then what about Fontevraud?"

Chapter 19

As they drove along the winding road that took them towards Fontevraud, Sally asked, "You took me for that wonderful tour of Yorkshire at Easter but why don't you talk to me about the Anglo-Saxons very much?"

"Well, to be honest, talking to you on our trip made me realise, that since I went to York, I was having trouble getting back into them," replied Ralph.

"How do you mean?"

"After I did my Ph.D., there weren't any vacancies for specialists and so I took posts teaching English Literature which usually had a limited life span which is how I ended up at the University of West Lancashire. I was always looking for the perfect job. I knew what I wanted and applied when any were advertised but the Jorvik post was the one I really wanted. I tried to keep up with all the latest news on the Anglo-Saxons but when I finally got to Jorvik, I was a bit out of touch and have had to put in a lot of hours catching up. Talking to you helped, and I am just about there, which is why the query about the future of my option threw me. Sorry, love."

"You've nothing to be sorry about. I thought the amount of work you were doing was par for the course."

"Now that I'm sorted and up to date, we can spend more time together."

"That will be great. So, this whole idea of me researching Robin of Redesdale was to stop me from getting in your way?"

"Well sort of. We were two independent people when we met, with our own ideas and routines. I mean I hadn't lived with anyone for quite a while and you had been on your own, I did wonder how we would fit together. And I wanted you to have your own interests."

"That's true. But surely all it takes is bit of give and take on both sides. We both cook when necessary and we both take out the rubbish. You help me change the beds and have been known to do a bit of ironing, and you're a wiz with the Hoover and what about your Shepherd's pie? What more can a girl ask for?"

"You mean that you have found me to be domesticated?"

"Yes, sorry, love, you are no longer a feral young man."

"Oh, heavens. Where did my misspent youth go to?"

They reached Fontevraud, and parked the car in the gothic car park, within its ornamental gateway, which appeared to be part of the Abbey. By now, it was getting towards time for a late lunch, so they walked to the square and looked at the menus available before deciding where to eat. The town was very busy, and they had to wait for a table. After a lunch of quiche and fruit, they crossed the square to the entrance to the Abbey grounds. The admission booth gave them a surprise in that on production of the tickets they had bought at Chinon gave them a discount on the entrance fee here.

They passed through the modern glass doors and into the medieval world of Fontevraud. Opposite them was the vast Abbey, which they reached by descending a wide staircase. Inside the church was its amazing spacious nave with, in the centre, the four funeral effigies of the Plantagenets that they had come to see. The painted effigies, of Henry II, his wife Eleanor of Acquitaine, their son, Richard I Coeur de Lion (Minus his heart which is in Rouen), and Isabella of Angouleme, the second wife of King John, who had gone back to France after her husband's death, lay on the floor of the nave of the church. Here they were buried, monarchs of England, far from home, but in their native land. Sally stood and pondered on them, as Ralph looked further around the church. She joined him and together they wandered into the cloisters and looked in some of the adjacent rooms. Fontevraud is a huge place reflecting its importance, to both England and France, in the Middle Ages.

"Thank you for bringing me," said Sally, as she kissed Ralph on the cheek. "That has been absolutely fantastic."

As they drove away from the town, Ralph added an item to their earlier discussion.

"I also began to wonder if you had made the right decision to marry me."

"Why on earth would you think that?"

"Well, you are so well organised, I wasn't sure that there was a place for me in your life."

"Look, my darling, for a start I may have appeared well-organised but I can assure you it was chaotic underneath the facade. Also, as you have so rightly stated on numerous occasions, I am a woman who knows her own mind. So, I will tell you here and now that if I, repeat I, decide that I made a mistake in marrying you, I will let you know straight off. No messing. So, until that never to be reached day, I can assure you, I did not make a mistake and have never been happier. Although to be honest, I did get a bit anxious when Marsha hove into view. I just hope all that is now behind us."

"Yes precious, Marsha has seriously disappeared into the past as far as I'm concerned. You have nothing to fear there. Following the dinner party from hell, she is definitely yesterday's news."

"Stop the car at the next parking spot," suggested Sally. "I feel like a kiss and cuddle after that or at least a stretch of the legs."

When they finally halted in a rest area, they left the car to sit on one of the picnic benches.

"Do you know?" Sally asked. "I feel as though I have lived my whole life in the last two days. Not only that with you I have come home." And she kissed her husband.

That evening over dinner at their hotel in Tours, Sally asked, "Where are we going now?"

"Where would you like to go? I thought we could go to Blois and stay the night and look at the Chateau, I believe it is amazing and then wander home. Unless you have somewhere else you would like to go."

"Well, Richard III came to France, you know, only the once as far as I am aware. He came with his brother, in I think, 1475 to fight the French but Edward was bought off at the Treaty of Picquigny. But it's up near Amiens. Would that be too far out of our way?"

"We'll get the maps out and work out a route. Following our change of plans when we came on our honeymoon, I only booked a one-way ticket this time, and left the return journey open. So, we could go back from a different port to Caen if we wanted to."

Together they looked at the map, and the route they would have to take to get to Picquigny, and after much discussion, decided that it was a step too far on this occasion. So, for this holiday, when so much had been clarified between them, they continued to explore the Loire Valley before returning to Caen and home.

Chapter 20

The Wednesday following their return from France, even though, technically, it was still during the university vacation, Sally made her way into the Gisburn Archive. Ralph accompanied her to the university as he wanted to check his mail. The greeting Sally received from Dr Fisher was most unexpected.

"Sally, lovely to see you back, did you have wonderful holiday?"

As Sally was only a volunteer, this was most unexpected. She assured him that she had had a most enjoyable holiday, and was now ready to take up the reigns of the project again.

"That is indeed good to know," said Dr Fisher. "But first we have something to show you. Knowing your interest in all things medieval, this item has now been deposited with us. It has been thoroughly examined while you have been away though we knew that you would be interested."

He took her into his office, in fact the room where Sally had been first interviewed months before. On the desk was the usual acid free box, in which documents and items for preservation where housed. He lifted the lid, and drew back the acid free paper covering, to reveal a brown leather pouch. He gave Sally a pair of cotton gloves, and putting on a pair himself, he lifted the pouch out of the box. He handed it to Sally who examined it, and noticed the writing on the outside. She looked at this carefully.

"Have you deciphered this?" she asked.

"Yes. It seems to be a warning or even a curse."

"Goodness," said Sally. "Have you opened it and brought the curse down on the Gisburn?"

"Well, we have opened it and so far, we have been quite safe. There is a letter inside, which knowing your interest in the Conyers we knew that you would want to see."

"Hang on a minute, I am only an amateur, surely an expert would be better?"

"Yes, they would, and they will get their turn in time but we thought that you should be one of the first."

"That is very kind of you."

Dr Fisher opened the pouch, turned the flap back, stiff with age it creaked softly and revealed the document within. He gently removed it to show the seal which, though broken, could easily be seen. The document was written on paper and had been folded twice across, opened out, it revealed a letter signed and dated.

"Have you read it?" asked Sally.

"Yes, and it makes very interesting reading," replied Dr Fisher. "In fact, if what it says is true the whole history of the late Middle Ages will have to be re-written."

"Why what does it say?"

"We've read it," said Dr Fisher. "But I'm going to let you find out what it says for yourself. You can take as long as you like. Make notes but because it has not been published or advertised yet, please keep it to yourself."

"Can I tell Ralph?"

"Yes but it goes no further for the time being. We still have tests to make on it, to find out if the paper and the pouch date from the time they purport to be from. Only when we are quite sure that it is genuine, will we tell the world."

"But in the meantime, you trust me with it? What about the curse?"

"I think the curse, if it is one, will only concern the people to whom the letter was originally sent."

"What does the curse say?" asked Sally.

"As far as we can tell, it says something along the lines of 'Cursed be he who opens this as it will bring down the crown of England'," replied Dr Fisher.

"Wow!" said Sally. "That's a bit strong. So now you think the danger is passed?"

"Yes. I'll leave you with it." Leaving Sally in the room with the letter, he went back to his office.

Left alone Sally began to peruse the letter. The writing, now brown with age, had probably been written in black or very dark brown ink, and Sally knew that even the type of ink used could be dated. Ink at the period of the Middle Ages, was made of oak galls which faded to brown with age. The writing was faded in places and Sally had a difficulty reading the odd word here and there, though most of it was legible. She opened her pad of paper and with a pencil, began to copy word for word and letter by letter leaving gaps where she could not make out the text. Obviously, she tried to make sense of it as she went along but tried to get the spelling and the words right to start with. By the time she had reached the end, it was two hours later and she realised that she was hungry. Leaving the letter on the desk, she went to Dr Fisher's office, where she found Ralph talking to him.

"Are you waiting for me?" she asked.

"Well, yes and no," Ralph replied. "I did come to find you but Stanley said that you were engrossed with what you were doing, so I left you too it."

"Did he tell you what it was?"

"No. He said you would do that in your own good time. I have been telling him about our holiday though."

"I've left everything as it was," Sally said to Stanley Fisher. "Is it all right if I take my notes home, or would it be better to leave them here?"

"How did you get on?"

"Well, I got most of it, but I shall have to have another go if that is all right with you?"

"Yes, when? Next week?"

"Can I come back tomorrow?"

"The sooner, the better. Leave your notes here overnight then. We'll see you in the morning."

"Thank you so much for letting me have a look at the document. I think I shall have to do some reading in the meantime. So, I'll be back tomorrow."

Ralph and Sally said farewell to Dr Fisher, and made their way out of the Gisburn. Sally had a bounce in her step, and Ralph realised that she had found her calling. He had not seen her so enthused for a long time and was delighted to see it.

"What did you find?" he asked. "Stanley told me that the Gisburn had been given a document of importance, and that you would find it particularly interesting. Was it about Robin of Redesdale?"

"Not exactly, and I will tell you about it when I'm quite sure what it is. Probably after I've had another look at it tomorrow. It is definitely significant." With that, Ralph had to be content for the moment.

Sally was very thoughtful all through lunch and gathered together quite a pile of her own books to look through, before her return to the Gisburn in the morning. She wanted to know as much as she could about what she was looking at.

Ralph gave her some space, and left her too her researches while he got in touch with Tom Williams to talk about their forthcoming climbing holiday.

Chapter 21

The following morning Sally rang the Public Library, to tell them that she was unable to go in for her normal shelf tidying session and made her way back to the Gisburn Archive. Ralph said that he would follow so that they could have lunch together. Actually, he was dying to find out what the mystery was all about. Knowing how long it had taken to solve his own mystery he knew that this one, if it was as much of a mystery, it might take some time to resolve. But he wanted to know.

As soon as she arrived, Stanley Fisher took her through to the search room with the document and her notes laid out. Again, she perused the document and tried to make a fair copy. After her research of the night before, she was able to decipher it and made a copy which satisfied her.

To Sir John Conyers
Late the Highe Sheriff of Yorkshire

To my good cousin and counsellor we greet you well. Your embassy has arrived here with your good wishes and enquiries concerning our well-being. I send this present to assure you that we are in good health as we trust God will keep us so. You ask how it was that we came into Burgundy and I propose to set down the way of it for your private use.

Following the death of the late King our father and the discovery of his prior betrothal before his marriage to our mother we were deprived of our rank by our uncle. My brother the late king Edward V and I were visited by our uncle who came to us in the Tower of London and explained that for our security and that of the realm we should remain private until it was safe to depart.

Our brother the king had been attended by doctor Argentine died at night and Sir James Tyrell was sent to remove him and arrange a privy burial at Windsor with our father. Sir James then came and took us out from the Towere to his house at Gipping where our mother came before we came into Burgundy to the safety of our aunt the Duchess.

Following the death of the King our uncle and the withdrawal of the Act which had made him King, Tudor gave us back our rights and on marrying our sister Elizabeth the Duchess of Burgundy thought it wise to send us into Spain to the house of Sir Edward Brampton where we stayed for several years before returning to Burgundy and the comfort of the Burgundian court.

We write this in gratitude for the service you have given our house in the past and which is now ceased. The cause of the Houses of York and Plantagenet is lost and we wish to live as quietly as world will allow.

Ricardus Shrewsbury

If what the document said was true, then much of what had been written about the fate of the so-called Princes in the Tower was false supposition. But was the writer genuinely Richard the younger son of Edward IV, or was it a fake produced at a later date to undermine the reign of the Tudors? There would have to be extensive investigation before the authenticity of the document could be established.

Sally took her fair copy of the letter, and was about to go into Dr Fisher's office, when she had a good look at the pouch for the first time. It had an envelope flap on which there seemed to be writing. Looking closely at it she peered at the writing, faded though it was. No, it was too faded to see what it said but there appeared to be some kind of a signature at the end. Leaving the pouch and the letter where they were, she went into Dr Fisher's office.

Again, there was Ralph waiting for her.

"Well," she said, "have you found out what it is all about?"

"I think so," Sally replied, giving her fair copy to Dr Fisher. "Is this what you made it out to be?"

Dr Fisher looked over her writing. "Yes. That's what we found," he said. "Now you can see why it has to remain confidential for the moment."

"Go on tell me what it is," demanded Ralph. His impatience was getting the better of him.

Sally looked at Dr Fisher. "Can I tell him?" she asked.

"Go on. He won't understand it as it is way out of his period but tell him anyway," joked Dr Fisher.

"Well, this appears to be a letter written by the younger of the so-called Princes in the Tower, in which he explains the death of his brother, the proclaimed Edward V, and his own removal, or escape from the Tower of London on the orders of his uncle, Richard III."

"Why do you say 'appears'?" asked Ralph.

"Because at the moment there is no evidence that it is genuine, and dates from the period in which it is supposed to have been written. It could be a fake."

"But if it is genuine what difference will that make?"

"All the difference in the world. The whole legend for the last 500 and odd years has been based on information, which was given by Sir Thomas More, in his history of the reign of Richard III, that Sir James Tyrell murdered the boys on Richard's orders because they were an inconvenience to him, which led to Shakespeare's play and into popular memory."

"So, I presume that the whole thing will have to be authenticated," said Ralph. "Will the Archive do that?"

"Yes, my colleagues and I will undertake that part of the enquiry. We can undertake the scientific investigation into the age of the paper, ink, handwriting, and the age of the leather pouch which it was given to us in," replied Dr Fisher.

"Will you do that?" asked Sally.

"Yes. Also, we will have to investigate the way the pouch came into the possession of the person who gave it to us. Where did they get it from etc?"

"Can I be involved in that?" said Sally in a very small tentative voice. "As you know I have done some research into finding out about someone's ancestors."

"I think we can let you be involved at this stage because of your knowledge, and also your interest in the period. We don't have a member of the Richard III Society on the staff."

"Thank you very much," said a grateful Sally.

"In fact, we are a bit stretched in staff numbers at the moment, so I think we had better hire you as a consultant for an agreed fee, and see how we get on. How would that suit you?"

"To be honest, I am rather overwhelmed," she replied. Sally looked at Ralph. He nodded at her.

"Go for it," he said.

"Right," said Sally. "When do you want me to start?"

"Come next Wednesday as usual and we can work out a plan of campaign." They all shook hands and Sally almost danced out of the Archive. Ralph had to hold her hand very tightly to stop her floating into the stratosphere. May be this was what she was meant to be doing.

Ralph thought, *I'd better read a book or two about all this so I will know what Sally is talking about.*

Chapter 22

During the next week, Sally wanted to keep to her usual routine but on Tuesday warned the public library that she might have to take a break from assisting with the self-tidying. As it was only a voluntary occupation, they were happy for her when she told them that she had got a project to follow up but hoped to come back in the future if it did not become permanent.

At home, she realised that Ralph was busy reading but what surprised her more was that he was reading her books on the Princes in the Tower. She challenged him on it.

"Hey up, love," she said, "are you getting interested in this?" as she indicated the book he was reading.

"Mm, yes," he said as he emerged from the page. "I thought that I had better find out what it was all about, so that I knew what you are talking about. I know you've been interested in the period since we met but you don't talk about it much."

"Well, I'm only an amateur," replied Sally. "And you're a professional academic and I didn't like to lock horns with you. It might spoil my enjoyment of the subject."

"Oh, darling, did you really think that of me?" he asked.

"Well, no not really, but there is so much sometimes, bad tempered argument about it, that I did not really want to know what you thought."

"I didn't know that I came over so heavy handed, you should have told me."

"I thought you might tease me, and then I would get upset," replied Sally.

"I know I've teased you about Richard III but only in fun. If I had realised that it was so important to you, I would never have teased you about it."

"I know that now," she said. "It was in the beginning when we first got to know each other; it was just something that I wasn't sure how you would take it. Then when you suggested me doing a project, and we talked about it and I started looking at Robin of Redesdale, that seemed fine and non-controversial but the fate of the Princes is another ball game."

"Look, I'm happy if you're happy," was all he finally said. It was later in the week just before her next meeting at the Gisburn, that Sally noticed a slight change in Ralph.

"What's the matter?" she asked.

"Nothing."

"Go on, I'm sure there's something."

"How much time is this research going to take up?" he asked.

"At the moment I don't know," was the reply. "Why?"

"Will you be out of the house for long?"

"Come on what's bothering you?"

"I've just realised that I like you being at home when I get back from the Jorvik, and that if this project takes off you might not be at home so much."

"Are you getting jealous?"

"Well, not of the project but of losing you to it."

"If you can remember way back in the days when I was working at West Lancs University, we managed to get together as often as possible, so why can't we do that again now?"

"Put like that, I can see I've lost the plot. I forgot a working wife would only have limited time at home."

"You've always helped with the chores," said Sally. "If you could make the odd meal if I am going to be late that would help, and we can keep in touch by text and phone. I'm sure we can manage. Look, you don't think that I am going to neglect you in favour of the project, do you?"

"I was a bit miffed, when I saw how excited you were, when we came out of the Gisburn last week. You hadn't been like that since we got married."

"Well, getting married was the last time I had something to write home about. Look, darling, no matter how excited or interested I get in a project, you are my only love. I love you so much and I would never neglect you. In fact, if you only knew how much I love every bit of you except, perhaps the little toe on you left foot." He now knew that everything was OK between them.

"What's wrong with the little toe on my left foot?"

"Not a lot," replied Sally. "But I did not want you to think that you were perfect. I couldn't live with perfection, so I had to find fault with something, and

I thought that the little toe on you left foot was the safest bit. I actually rather like the rest of you." Now he knew she was joking and laughed.

"I do love you so much," he said. "I suppose I was a bit jealous of you spending time with another man, I mean men, I mean Princes. Damn, I think I was just a bit jealous that you had found an alternative to me."

"Never an alternative, just a glance to the side." Sally kissed him and he kissed her. Problem solved.

Chapter 23

The following Wednesday morning, Sally was all ready for the day. She had looked at all the books she owned which might give her some clue as to what she was to do next. That is when she could find them. Inexplicably several of them were missing and she ran them to earth in Ralph's study. Over the week, she had become quite an expert on what was supposed to have happened to the Princes in the Tower.

Because it was still vacation time, there was plenty of space available in the university car park, so she drove to the Gisburn Archive. Inside, Susan Hartley greeted her and took her through to Dr Fisher.

"Sally, I've got some good news for you. The board has agreed to you assisting with this project and there will be a fee at the end of it based on the fee that family history researchers charge." He named an amount.

"I would only expect to get that amount if I was successful," said Sally.

"No, I think you will find that is the fee for the work done, whether or not you are successful, besides it has been agreed. If I were you, I'd take it."

"Well, I know that I shall enjoy doing the research. What can you tell me about the donation?"

"It was given by Miss Alice Atherton who lives over at Pickering. She did not say much when she brought it in. She just came in. Sometimes donors get in touch first and ask if we would like something, but not this time. Apparently, the object had been in her family for quite a long time, and as she was getting on a bit, and with no one in her family left to leave it to, she thought we were the safest place for it."

"So, we don't really know very much about its provenance then?"

"No. We will have to go over to Pickering to see her and find out much more. In the meantime, we have been examining the pouch and managed to decipher most of the writing on it. It makes very interesting reading." Dr Fisher produced a sheet of paper, on which was written, "To my family, do not open this, do not read the contents for they will bring down kings and lead to the end of my line."

"Goodness," said Sally. "I can quite see what the writer was getting at. Does that mean that no one has read the letter since it was received in 1489 or whenever?"

"It looks like it but we will know more after we have been to Pickering. Susan here has made an appointment with Miss Atherton for next Wednesday if you are free to accompany us, we will go over to see her."

The following Wednesday Ralph dropped Sally at the Gisburn, and Dr Fisher, Susan Hartley and Sally bundled into one car and set off for Pickering.

On their arrival, Miss Atherton took them into her small but neat, sitting room at the front of the terraced house. She offered them a cup of tea and when it arrived, accompanied by buttered scones, they sat down to ask the all-important questions.

"The document you deposited with us," began Dr Fisher, "can you tell us a bit about its history?"

"Why is there something wrong with it?" she asked.

"No. It's just that at this time we need to know a little more about it."

"Well, it was given to my father by his father, and told never to read it, as the contents were such that they could bring down the wrath of the crown on the family."

"So, you never looked at? Did you even have a peep?"

"No. Definitely not. Father would have been turning in his grave."

"Can you tell us how it came into your family then?"

"As far as I know, it has always been in the family going right back to at least William Allanson my ten times great grandfather. The name has changed over the years of course, as sometimes it came down through the female line."

"You've traced your family tree?" asked Sally butting in.

"Actually, one of my cousins did many years ago. He is dead now and there is no one left to leave it to which is why I brought it to the Gisburn."

"So, it goes back to William Allanson. Who was he?"

"He owned Crayke Castle in the middle of the seventeenth century, during the Civil War."

"So, you think that he found it at Crayke Castle?"

"His son Charles restored the castle before the diocese of Durham got the castle back in about 1667. He must have found it then and kept it. As far as the family knew, no one ever looked inside the leather pouch."

"Why?"

"Well, according to family legend, there was writing on the pouch which read: 'If this pouch is opened the Kingdom will Fall and the wrath of God will be visited on the descendants of the Conyers.' Charles Allanson married into the Conyers family, so it has always been left strictly alone."

"You mean, that you thought that it was cursed?" asked Sally.

"Something like that," replied Miss Atherton. "Why have you looked at it?"

"Yes," said Sally, "and it made very interesting reading."

"Why? What did it say?"

"I don't know whether I should tell you as it might invoke the curse."

"Go on, I won't be actually reading it if you tell me what it says. The wrath of God has not yet come down on us."

"I think," said Sally, "that when it was written it probably would have if the contents of the pouch had become known."

"Go on, Tell me."

Sally looked at Dr Fisher for permission. He nodded in assent. "This is your story," he said.

"The pouch contains a letter written in about 1488, not long after the Battle of Stoke Field when Lambert Simnel was captured by Henry VII, and confessed to being a fraud, and not being one of the Princes in the Tower. It would appear the Sir John Conyers had sent an envoy to Flanders, to find out the truth about the imposture. As a loyal servant of the Yorkist dynasty, he wanted to know what had happened to the Princes. The letter is supposed to be from the real Prince Richard of Westminster, the younger son of Edward IV, and explains what happened to himself and his brother, and how he now wishes to live quietly away from political turmoil."

"So why would the letter be cursed?"

"I don't think that the letter itself is or was cursed, just the fact of its existence and knowledge about what it contained, would have brought the owner close to the gallows or the block. Sir William Stanley was executed in 1495 for simply saying that if Perkin Warbeck was Richard of Westminster, he would not oppose him. Actually, by that time Sir John Conyers had been dead for about five years, so it could have been his grandson who wrote the warning, and gave the pouch to the Durham Diocese at Crayke."

"So why have you come to see me?"

"We wanted to know where the document had come from in order to discover its authenticity. It might be a fake but if what it says is true, then parts of the history books will have to be re-written."

"Is that the end of it then?"

"Oh, no. We shall have to authenticate it with all the tests we can muster to find out its age. So far, with your information we now know a little more about its history and where it has been over the last few years."

"What kind of tests?"

"We will need to date the paper, the ink, and the age of the pouch."

"Please will you let me know what you find out?"

"Yes, of course."

They took their leave.

Chapter 24

On the way home, Sally pondered on what she had learned. Obviously, Miss Atherton believed that she was descended from William Allanson, and that the pouch had been found at Crayke. She knew, from doing family history, that it was very easy to make assumptions about you own ancestry and make it fit into a pre-existing pattern and that this could lead you up blind alleys, and into finding completely wrong ancestors.

"I think," she said, "that I am going to have to go back and have another talk to Miss Atherton. I think that it will be best if I can get all the connections on her family tree just in case her cousin made a leap of faith about their ancestors. Also, find any connections between Crayke and the Conyers family."

"I thought you would begin to have ideas before we got back to York," said Dr Fisher. "When do you want to start?"

"Straightaway. I'll ring her tomorrow and get all the information she can give me about her family, and then I can look them up on the censuses and the births, marriages and deaths, and find the chain. Will there be money for expenses in the budget? Certificates can be expensive. The registers go to Southport where you can't actually look at them. If they are still kept locally, I might get a look but Yorkshire is a big place. It depends if the family moved around a lot."

"At the moment, I think it would be best to see how much it is all going to cost before I commit the Gisburn to a great deal of expense."

"That's OK," said Sally. "I'll get as far as I can via the internet and the censuses before we get into certificates. There might not be many; anyway, the real fun will start when we get back before civil registration, and an element of guesswork can come in. Parish registers are what we will need then."

"As you know, we have quite a collection of Yorkshire ones in the Gisburn, so that is not a problem."

"Have you got copies of the old International Genealogical Index on microfiche?"

"We used to have," replied Dr Fisher. "I think we put it into store when more material became available on the internet. Why?"

"I am a bit old fashioned, and I have found it very useful with my own family history. I know that it is out of date but I still think that it is a useful starting point."

"When we get back, we'll have a hunt and see what we have got."

"When I've got some names, I shall need wills, well I know about them. I shall also want anything about the Conyers family, and also Crayke Castle."

"Only a short list." Dr Fisher laughed. "I can see you are going to keep us busy."

"I am sorry." Sally smiled. "It's such a long time since I got my teeth into anything that I'm burbling a bit. I'm really going to enjoy this."

"Good. What's Ralph think of all this?"

"He doesn't mind me researching something and I think he is secretly doing background reading, so he knows what I'm talking about."

"Will he keep it confidential until we are sure of our ground?"

"Oh, I am sure of that."

Chapter 25

During the following week, Sally wrote to Miss Atherton telling her what she needed to know in order to go further with the verification of the document. She also asked if she had a copy of her late cousin's research, into the family tree, which she could borrow. While waiting for a reply, Sally read up all she could about the Allanson family and Crayke Castle and its importance to the Diocese of Durham.

At the end of the next week was August Bank Holiday, and Ralph's climbing holiday with the old gang from Leeds University. This time they were going to Glen Coe in Scotland and were camping on the site of the village which was destroyed by the Campbells in 1692. Sally was staying in York and as she had made no plans for a holiday with her old friend Lynne, she had initially been content to spend the time looking at York's many attractions. However, when Lynne heard of this, she immediately invited herself to stay with Sally so that they could have a girls' holiday of their own. So, on Saturday, after Ralph had left, Lynne arrived from Sheffield. The two old friends had spent many holidays together in the years leading up to Sally's marriage but since then they had not been as close and this was an ideal opportunity to re-bond without the interference of men. Lynne had initially thought that Sally had jumped into marrying Ralph too quickly but she now saw that her old friend had made a good move.

They spent the week looking at medieval York and visited both the Richard III Experience at Monk Bar, and so as to not show any bias, also went to Micklegate Bar to see the Henry VII Experience. Sally also told her friend that she was looking into the history of Crayke Castle, and so they had a day out and went and had a look at it. The run along the A19 with the Hambleton Hills ahead of then always lifts the spirits as does the view of the Kilburn White Horse. They came back via Newburgh Priory, believed by many to be the last resting place, of Oliver Cromwell, and to Coxwold, home to Shandy Hall the house of

Laurence Sterne author of 'Tristram Shandy', believed to be the first English novel. Then back to York.

On the way back Lynne, who was driving because Ralph had taken the Armstrong car to Scotland, said, "So what is all this about?"

"Well, I've got myself some research work which involves Crayke," replied Sally.

"What is it you're doing?" asked Lynne.

"I am looking into a family which once lived at Crayke, which is why I wanted to go to see the castle. It's going to mean looking at censuses and parish registers, trying to trace the family back through the centuries."

"That sounds rather boring. Are you sure you really want to do it. I know you were involved with the Family History Society in Ormsbury but thought that you had come to your senses when you got married and came to York."

Sally laughed. "O, Lynne," she said. "I'll never come to my senses. You've known me…How long is it? Nearly 25 years and have you ever known me do anything you thought was sensible?"

"That's true. I thought you were mad getting married. I've managed quite nicely, thank you, without."

"Yes but I'm not you. I've gone my own way. I know, when you went down Sheffield University, I thought I'd lost you but you've stayed in touch all these years, even though you thought I was mad. But I've enjoyed myself. To be honest, I never thought I would get married but now I have, it's great fun."

"Don't tell me that you are thinking of having a family?"

"Well, yes we are, at least we are working on it."

"Oh, well if you produce a sprog, I'm not going to be Aunty Lynne I can tell you now. I am far too young."

"You're the same age as me, you nut."

"Anyway, how are you going to manage an infant and your project?"

"I'll manage," replied Sally with confidence. "I've been a librarian. I can multitask."

By this time, they were driving along the York bypass and nearing home.

"You'd think," said Lynne, "that if you are the same age as me, which I doubt, that you would have more sense. Your husband will go off you if you, start spending more time with a sprog, than with him."

"I know there is a danger," reassured Sally. "But I've got it all worked out. It's all to do with time management."

They pulled into Sally's drive, climbed out of the car and went into the house.

"Besides," said Lynne, "if you have a family where will you put me when I come to stay?"

"You mean you still want to come and visit us after all you've said, about me marrying Ralph?"

"We have been friends for far too long for me to let a little thing, like you being married, come between us."

"Gee, thanks."

"If you can put up with him, then so can I. Particularly, if it is only in small doses."

They enjoyed the rest of the week and on Friday evening, Ralph came home. A pleasant evening was spent, and Lynne managed to curb her tongue before she left for home on Saturday morning.

"Have you had a good time?" asked Ralph as Lynne's car disappeared down the road.

"Yes, we did," replied Sally. "I took her to Crayke and Coxwold, as well having a good exploration of York. It was good seeing her again after such a long time. She says she will come and visit us while you are here, if that is OK."

"I've no problem with her. I just could never fathom why she did not like me."

"She thought that you would cramp my style, and turn me into a housewife, and that I would lose my independence."

"Some people are funny, aren't they? Fancy her thinking that I could have any influence over you!"

"How did your holiday go?"

"Very well. Once we had got over the initial getting together again. The usual gripes got aired but once we put them to bed, we had a great time. I was glad that I had gone back to wall climbing otherwise I would have been very stiff after a day on the rock face. But it was good. Tim asked after you. He has sorted out his problems and got another job, so everything was well with him."

"I'm so glad. The poor man was so down when he came to see us that time."

"You worked wonders there. Actually, I've asked him to drop in on his way home if that is not a problem. I know he wanted to talk to you in person."

"Oh, goodness when will he come? Does he want to stay? I'll have to get a bed ready." Sally was in a flap.

"He will call as he gets near. He stayed an extra night in Scotland, and he's not going to stay, so calm down. In the meantime, have you done any more with your project?" Ralph was interested.

"No. I'm waiting for Miss Atherton to get back to me, and then I can really get going."

"Term starts soon and there will lots of meetings for me, so I'm not going to be much help for a while."

"As long as the rubbish gets put out, we'll cope," said Sally.

"Is that all I'm good for?"

"No. But it will help to keep this show on the road."

Tim rang at 6:30 to say he was at Tadcaster and would be with them soon. It was not long before he arrived and took them both out for a meal before continuing his journey south. *It was good to see him again,* thought Sally, *and looking much better than the last time she had seen him.* Before mid-night, he set off again and rang the next day to say he had got home safely.

Chapter 26

On the following Monday, which was 3 September, Sally received the letter she had been waiting for. Miss Atherton had found a copy of the Family History which her cousin Henry had produced, and was ready for Sally to visit and copy the relevant information. She also gave Sally her phone number, so Sally immediately rang her to arrange a visit. That evening she told Ralph that she would need the car to go to Pickering on the following Wednesday.

"How long will it take?" he asked.

"The visit shouldn't take long but I may be away most of the day. Why, do you need the car?"

"No but I thought I might come with you, if you don't mind."

"I don't. In fact, I would be glad of the company. But I ought to warn Miss Atherton, that you will be coming. She has been very good about letting the Archive staff go *en masse* but might not like another stranger."

"Fair enough."

"Why do you want to go?"

"Pure curiosity and I want to see you at work."

"In that case, I'm not sure you should come along. If she has all the relevant certificates, I will want to photograph them, so I will know who I am looking for."

"Can you at least tell me what this project will involve as far as you are concerned?" At last, he had asked what she was going to get up to.

"Well, I need to know that she is who she says she is, and then prove a family connection with Crayke Castle. I need to prove that she is really descended from William Allanson. I looked the history of Crayke up on the internet, and it was originally part of the dioceses of Durham which as you know (which means I am about to tell you), was a Prince Bishopric and had special privileges. It could easily have become the depository for such an explosive letter. In the depths of an ecclesiastical house, it would be quite safe from the questing minions of an angry or interested King Henry either one. The castle was slighted and sold by the Parliamentarians to Sir William Allanson during the Civil War. He was a York man who had been the MP and Mayor of York. His son Charles restored it and in 1667, it was given back to the see of Durham, and was leased out as a farmhouse. The theory that I am working on, at the moment, is that the document and pouch had been hidden in the castle sometime in the fifteenth century, and found by Charles Allanson, during the repair and restoration of the building. He then kept it when the manor was given back to Durham. The pouch and its contents were then handed down through his descendants, until it came to Miss Atherton. She now has no living relatives on her father's side of the family. The cousin who looked at her family tree was on her mother's side. All I have to do is prove the connection."

"Not asking a lot then!"

"So, there are two lines I have to trace. Firstly, I have to prove the descent of Miss Atherton from Charles Allanson and secondly, I have to find a connection between the Conyers of Hornby and Crayke, to find a reason why the document would be there in the first place. Next week is when I start from this end. It means looking at birth and marriage certificates, following the trail back to 1837, to the start of Civil Registration. At the same time, I will have to look at Parish Registers to find Charles Allanson's descendants, and at some point, hope lines will meet."

"Do you know, I would dearly love to join you but I can see that it is going to be a lot of hard work, so I think I will leave you too it. But keep me up to date on how you are getting on. Will you, love?"

"Yes, of course. You will hear all my gripes. I know you will. Your job will be to keep me balanced."

"Will do. I know how complicated it got when I was doing my Ph.D. and I think that this is going to be just as tough."

"Thank you for that. It has really cheered me up."

"Look, I know what hard work went into solving my mystery, so I am sure that you will have no trouble."

"It's just a case of tracking the sources and references down. The trouble is I am a bit out of practice."

"You'll be fine," said the ever-supportive husband.

So, on the Wednesday of the following week, Sally drove alone to Pickering.

Alice Atherton was waiting when Sally arrived promptly at 10 am. The kettle was on, and the scones were waiting. The paperwork that she had found was laid out on the dining table, ready for Sally to peruse. But first was a cup of tea.

"Thank you so much for letting me look at this record," said Sally. "You do realise," she continued, "that I am going to check all your cousin's findings. The problem with tracing family history is that there is so much information available now on the internet. Also, people make their family trees available as well. Unfortunately, sometimes other researchers add their own information which may not, either be accurate, or relate directly to the family they have found, which confuses the issue. I'm afraid I found instances of this when I was doing my own family. So, while I can accept the documentation that you know from your own experience, I will have to check anything that dates from earlier years."

They made a start. Miss Atherton had a copy of her own birth certificate which Sally took a photograph of, and then her parents' marriage certificate which had fathers' names on it, and then her father's and mother's birth certificates, which also gave their mothers' names. By this time, they had got back to before the 1911 census which would show the parents and siblings of them both. Miss Atherton was sure that the pouch had come from her father's side of the family, and so Sally concentrated on that. The cousin, Henry, had copied the census entries from the ancestry website and so was pretty confident that they were the right ones but Sally knew that she would have to check that there was not another family with similar ages, names and location before she could be sure that this was the right one. She followed the thread back to 1841 and photographed all the information. This is the earliest census available, and of course Civil Registration only began in 1837, so any information earlier than that would have to come from parish registers.

All this took a good deal of time up and when she had finished Sally thanked, Miss Atherton, and said that she hoped that she had not taken up too much of her time.

"Goodness, no," was the reply. "I've enjoyed having you here."

Chapter 27

The next time Sally went into the Gisburn Archive on Tuesday 18 September, she went to find Stanley Fisher.

"Have you had the results of the scientific analysis yet?" she asked.

"Yes, and very interesting they have proved to be," he said. "The paper, ink and leather all date to the last half of the fifteenth century give or take 30 years, so there seems to be some grounds for believing that they are authentic. However, we shall await the results of your research before we can be absolutely certain."

Sally made a start on checking Alice Atherton's ancestry that very day. She had already printed the certificates, and all the other data she had collected from her visit to Miss Atherton. She had also been to the public library and checked on the censuses. She had not found another family with the same names as Alice's ancestors, and so was fairly certain that the information that Cousin Henry had found was correct. To give herself a break from gazing at a computer screen, she went into the Archive's catalogue to look for any documents which might relate to the family, such as wills, probates, court appearances, or indentures. Parish clerks' accounts might also mention the family but she would first have to find out which parish the family had been living in.

Ralph came to find her for lunch. She told him what she was doing and mentioned the results of the scientific tests, and after lunch she went back to the project. Now it was back to looking at the International Genealogical Index on Microfiche which the staff had thankfully discovered, at the back of the Archives. The entries usually finished in about the 1880s, so whilst there is an overlap with the Civil Registration, she still needed to know which parishes the family were resident in at the time. Gradually, she began to build up a picture of the family, its residences and its occupations, and by the time she finished for the day, she felt that she had achieved quite a lot.

That evening, when she got home, Ralph had made the dinner and put the rubbish out. *At this rate,* Sally thought, *we might manage to work in harmony.*

"Thank you for this," said Sally over a dinner of Ralph's signature dish, a shepherd's pie. "I know that while I have not had a job, I have been doing lots of household things which we managed to do between us when we were both working. But this had been really thoughtful of you."

"It was while I was cycling to the Jorvik this morning that I suddenly realised what you had been doing for me all these months. I mean while we were in Cleckheaton and I was commuting, you were rather left to take care of the house. Since we came here, I carried on expecting the same, as it was nice having someone to look after me but this morning, I realised that you need looking after too. So now that we are settled, I am going to do more about the house. I did it while I was on my own, before I met you, and I can do it again." Ralph suddenly took on his knight in shining armour persona and Sally laughed and hugged him.

After dinner, Ralph asked, "Please explain the significance of the results of the tests? I did not like to ask too much, whilst we in the senior common room because you know what big ears they have in there. Always ready to pounce on the latest piece of gossip."

"That's OK," replied Sally. "I did not want to launch into one of my hectic expositions in public anyway. It means," she continued, "that there is a 95% chance that the letter is genuine, in that all indications show that it dates from the right period. But the problem is, was it written by Richard of Shrewsbury/Westminster or was it written by someone else?"

"You mean it could still be a fake?"

"Oh, yes. It could have been written at any time, by someone out to cause trouble, during the last part of the fifteenth century, and still appear authentic. But any trouble would only be caused if it was found, and it wasn't. So, if it dates from the right time then it is probably genuine. So, all I have to do is to find a connection between Sir John Conyers and Alice Atherton."

"How are you going to do that?"

"Well, I have made a start. Today, I began checking the research that Alice's cousin, Henry, had done with tracing the family tree. I have also looked to see what sources there are at the Gisburn Archive, and I have also been to the library to look at the censuses and to confirm those. So, I am now back to 1841. Before that, I will have to look at parish registers and have arranged to look at the I.G.I. next time I go to the Gisburn."

"You keep taking about this I.G.I. What is it? You never mentioned it when you were tracing my family."

"It was useless when I was looking into your family because what I was doing was too new. Most of the information available dates to at least 100 years ago. The powers that be don't like making information available which might be about people who are still alive. So, the I.G.I. It is the International Genealogical Index and covers baptisms and marriages from parish registers up to the late nineteenth century. It was produced by the Church of Jesus Christ of the Latter-Day Saints for their own purposes but to my mind, is an invaluable tool for the family historian. It was produced on Microfiche, 6 by 4 inch, pieces of microfilm with pages of information on them. They were produced by county, so the Yorkshire microfiche cover the whole county from the beginning of the start of Parish Registers. They are also in alphabetical order so you can look for a name. Each baptism entry gives the names of the parents of the child and marriages give the names of both parties. It is now out of date because computers have taken over but I find it useful because you can track down whole families at one sitting. The parishes are also listed which means, now I know that the Gisburn has the IGI, I can check it out on site. There isn't as much direct information on the website. I know I'm old fashioned in this but I do like hard copy."

"I don't think I would ever argue with you over this. So, what else do you have to do?"

"Parish registers only started in the 1530s and then not everywhere. It was a product of the break with Rome and Henry VIII's need to know what his people were doing. So, for anything earlier than that I need to go back to the archives. I only need to go back to William Allanson for Alice's ancestors so I might work forward from him and see if the two threads meet."

Chapter 28

The autumn had come around again and the prospect of the community theatre starting again with a new production and Sally decided that she would take part again. This time there was no Jenny, who found that her shifts at the hospital did not make it easy to attend rehearsals, so Sally now much more confident than the previous year joined in with enthusiasm. The show that was planned was *Calamity Jane*; another show that Sally remembered from Ormsbury. Again, she was in the chorus, and was enjoying the singing.

One Saturday in the middle of October, after Sally had made her start on tracing the history of the document, and just before term proper began at the university, Sally and Ralph had a celebratory dinner. They had been living in York for a year and decided that it was time for a review of the year and the prospects for the future. They did this from time to time and the beginning of a new year seemed to be the right time.

They went down into York and had a meal at one of their favourite restaurants by the river and after eating, strolled for a while hand in hand before going back to the car and driving home. As they walked, they talked. The restaurant was too noisy for intimate confidential conversation but here in the open air they could talk comfortably.

"How are you feeling now?" Ralph asked. "This time last year you were suffering from job frustration and I occasionally feared for my skull."

"Idiot," replied Sally, "you were never in any real danger. I was more likely to take it out on the furniture or myself, like I did when I hurt my hand when I had glandular fever."

"I must admit I was quite surprised that you could be so aggressive with yourself."

"Actually, I surprised myself. Most things I take in my stride. Anyway, you will be pleased to learn that all that is now behind me. At least until next time!"

"You're feeling more settled now, love?"

"Yes, I have settled down, and now I have a routine, and a worthwhile task to do, I am feeling more like my old self. How are things with you?"

"Well now, I have been at Jorvik for a while I too am settled. It is much easier now we are living here, rather than having to commute from Clecky. I know I got a bit anxious about you not being at home when I got back but I am over that now too. I suppose it was silly of me, but I found I liked having you to come home to, made me feel young again with Mum at home when I got back from school. Silly I know."

"Sure is, I don't feel a bit like your mother." They stopped strolling and Ralph held Sally close. "No you're not," he said into her hair. Holding hands, they continued their walk.

"I'm not sure how long my job at Jorvik is going to last?" he said after a pause.

"Why? What's happened?"

"The meeting I went to the other day was a review of acceptances by new students. At the moment, numbers are holding up but there is a question mark over the department. It is an intellectually rigorous course, and students don't seem to want to be challenged now. We are looking at ways to make it more user-friendly but if we can't recruit, then we will either have to lose staff or close completely."

"I didn't think they could do that. I thought that Anglo-Saxon Studies was the whole purpose of the university."

"Yes, it is. That is why it was founded in the first place. But apparently, there is nothing to stop the powers that be from closing us if they so decide."

"It looks as though you are going to have to do that TV series that you were offered, to try to make the subject cool and relevant in today's age."

"I'm glad you've said that. It has come up in discussion, and I know that Jeremy Bond is in favour but it means contacting Marsha, and I didn't know how you would feel about that."

"If that is what it takes to keep the department going, then do it if you can. It could be that all publicity is good publicity."

Ralph pulled her to him and gave her a very passionate kiss right there on the river bank.

"Thank you, love," he said. "You have always been supportive but this maybe the end. Let's hope that Marsha has given up trying to get me back. I'm going nowhere if you aren't there."

Sally kissed him retuning his passionate embrace.

"Hey up, lass," Ralph gasped. "What's got into you?"

"It just came to me," Sally replied, "that we have never canoodled on a river bank and it's about time we did."

For some minutes, they kissed and cuddled in the shadow of the wharf buildings before the sound of footsteps approaching broke them apart.

"So now I've been canoodled," said Ralph. "I always wondered what it was like."

"You are an idiot," was the reply.

They held hands as they turned to walk back to the car and home.

"Do you know," he said, "one of the best things I found out this year has been that I have enjoyed working in the garden. After Stephen gave me some ideas and help laying down the lawn, I find that grubbing about in the soil, eases the burdens of the day."

"Oh, I'm so glad you feel like that, 'cos I do too," answered Sally. "Not having had a garden at Ormsbury, and only a small patch at Cleckheaton, I thought maybe I had lost the knack. Dad always did the garden at home and I never learned much but I have enjoyed planting things this year. Next year, I might even get to sit outside."

They reached the car. "You know," she said, "if you can help around the house while I am doing this project, we will manage. I mean the odd bit of hoovering and dusting and perhaps a bit of ironing, then I can concentrate on the project, and it will be finished quicker."

"You realised that I wasn't very domesticated when you married me. Remember the mugs."

"Yes, all 42 of them. Am I likely to forget, well, we got them washed and it never happened again, this will be the same."

"Anyway, as long as you don't go around checking to see if I've done the dusting, we will get along fine."

Chapter 29

It was three days later when Ralph came home from a departmental meeting at the university.

"I've done it," he said as he burst through the kitchen door to find Sally busy preparing the evening meal.

"Done what?" she asked.

"I tackled Jeremy about the idea of doing some television broadcasts to try to encourage more students to take up the course."

"What did he say?"

"He was in favour, of course. He had been getting suggestions from all quarters and has decided to let us put forward our ideas in the form of a seminar at the next department meeting. Apparently, some of the old guard are thinking that early retirement would suit them better, and would rather the department closed than go in for some new ideas. Anyway, Jeremy wants to give it a try, so I have to have some ideas ready to sell to the others by next week."

"So, what are you thinking?" Sally was busy chopping onions which made her eyes water.

"There's no need to cry about it," Ralph said. "I thought that I would suggest a series of programmes, which if they get through the department, I could then submit to the television company that Marsha kept pointing out to me."

"Have you had some thoughts?"

"Yes, as I was cycling home ideas kept popping into my head, so if you don't mind, I'll go down to the study and start writing them down."

"Good idea. Dinner will be ready in about an hour. I'll give you a shout."

After dinner, Ralph disappeared into his study again and Sally did not see him for the rest of the evening until he came to bed.

The next day she went to the Gisburn archive to continue her research, leaving Ralph alone in the house. When she came back in the early afternoon, she found three used mugs in the kitchen and Ralph missing. She went to look for him and found him in his study working feverishly over his computer. Beside him was a mug of tea and a flask.

"Have you had anything to eat?" she asked.

Ralph looked up. "Hello, darling," he said. "I don't think so."

Sally went back upstairs and made him a sandwich which she took down to him.

"How are you getting on?"

"Just a moment," he replied, "let me finish this. I'll come and tell you about it when I get it finished." Sally left him too it.

After a while, she heard Ralph coming upstairs from his study. She looked at him eagerly as he came into the kitchen.

"How have you got on?" she asked.

"Sorry about that, love," he replied. "I was on a roll and did not want to break off. I think that I have got a plan worked out. All I've got to do now is run it passed Jeremy. Perhaps you will have a look at it first to see if there are any glaring errors."

"Of course, I will. When do you want me to do it?"

"What about now?"

"OK with me."

"Right here goes. I have worked it out as a series of TV programmes but hopefully, it would also work as on-line course. It is only an outline of what is available to whet the appetite of prospective students. I thought that the whole department could be involved. I don't want to be the sole performer. Firstly, an overview of the whole Anglo-Saxon period up to the Norman invasion. Ted from History could do that. He does it for us now. Secondly: a look at the literature of the period. There is quite a lot available including Beowulf. Then a look at the daily life of an Anglo-Saxon family, then the archaeology and finds Sutton Hoo etc. and ship burials, the coming of Christianity and how life changed, medicine and health, next, the coming of the Vikings both Norse and Danish and lastly, the Norman Conquest. For me the crucial part is what was left after the conquest, particularly as the language survived despite William's best efforts to destroy all opposition in the harrying of the North. I've been trying to work out where to put the significant leaders, you know, King Alfred and Cnut, not forgetting significant women such as Aethelfled, a lady of the Mercians. In fact, I think that if anyone did the whole course, it would take three years!"

"Ha, ha," said Sally. "If you cover all that it sounds absolutely exciting. Can I do the course too?"

"Seriously, what do you think?"

"I think it's a great idea. I don't know what a TV company would think of it. But Marsha was right all those years ago, there is a gap in the market. There was a well-known historian who did a series about the Dark Ages years ago but nothing recently."

"Well, if you can't think of any serious errors or omissions, then I'll give it to Sid next week. I might also send it to Marsha to show to the right people."

"To be honest, I don't know enough about the period to comment on omissions but I do like the sound of it so far."

"Phew!" said Ralph. "I haven't got so keyed up for a long time. I think since my Ph.D. I was always having second thoughts about that. Thanks, love."

"You know I'll always support you in whatever you do. We'll just have to see how it goes. I suppose as far as getting students is concerned, it will depend on how enthused they are with the subject. I know that you found the romance of it exciting and of course there is the link with things like *Lord of the Rings* being set in this kind of period. Oh, and that TV series which we didn't see, *Game of Thrones*. That might encourage more students if they could see the link."

"Just another great idea from my lovely wife."

"Don't be daft."

Chapter 30

Following the visit that Ralph and Sally had made to Stephen and Jenny's house, Ralph and Stephen became allies in turning the piece of ground at the back of Ralph's house into a garden. As a result, Ralph would ring for advice and in return, Ralph would answer Stephen's queries about his Viking History. Stephen also learned some choice Anglo-Saxon oaths which he could use on appropriate occasions. Occasionally, Stephen might turn up if he was in the neighbourhood, to sample the contents of the man cave, or shed, known to both as 'The Mead Hall'. On one such occasion, in early autumn, when the sun was shining, Stephen had just called around, and was in the Mead Hall filling his beaker, when the garden gate opened, and Marsha came in.

Sally was upstairs in the lounge reading about Richard, Duke of Gloucester, and his contact with Hornby. The kitchen window was open to let in some of the warm autumn air.

Marsha did not see Stephen in the shed, and believes that she and Ralph are alone.

Ralph's looked up from contemplating the lawn and thinking profound thoughts about Anglo Saxon swear words. "What are you doing here?" he asked.

"I hear on the grape vine that you had come around to my way of thinking," she replied.

"But only about Anglo-Saxon programmes."

"No. It's much more than that. You need me."

"I'm grateful. In fact, we are all grateful for your help but we only need it for the future of the department."

"I'm talking about our future."

"No. My future is settled. I am where I want to be."

"Yes, with me."

"No. I've got Sally. She is what I want."

"She can't be. She's only a little person. A librarian for heaven's sake with an ordinary mind."

"Actually, she's pretty spectacular; you don't know the half of it."

"She can't even get a proper job. Nobody has ever heard of her."

"People will in time, I know it."

"But you can have me, and fame now."

"Thanks for the offer but I've been there; remember, I don't want to go back. I'm going forwards. Sally is my future. She's what I want. Can't you understand that?"

"You could be a household name."

"You offered me that once before. I didn't want it then. Celebrity is over-rated. I'm going to write my own books and my name will be remembered, if it is, through my work and not because I've been on the box."

"Oh you! You've no ambition. Here I am offering you the world and you're turning me down."

"That's right. I am. My one ambition was to be where I am right now. Doing what I am doing. The television thing is only to help me stay that way. I am with my Sally. You can't offer me anything better."

By now, the voices had got louder, and Sally heard them from above and crossed to the kitchen window to hear what was going on. She looked out and saw Marsha crossing the lawn towards the gate. In the shed doorway, Stephen was lurking, trying to look inconspicuous.

He came out. "Who was that?" he asked.

"An old friend of mine, Marsha Hamilton."

"Rather more than a friend, I think," was all that Stephen said.

"Yes but it was a long time ago."

"Does Sally know?"

"Oh yes! She knows and she understands."

"Well, if she does, she's one hell of a wife."

"I know, that's why I get so annoyed when Marsha shows up trying to interfere in my life."

"She wants you to go on TV? What would I give to be a TV gardener?"

"Yes but she wants me too. We were an item once and she wants a repeat. She had her chance and blew it; that sounds arrogant, damn! Can we change the subject? What about those daffodils? Actually, I have a better idea, how about some choice Anglo-Saxon oaths. I feel a few coming on."

106

Sally thoughtfully went back to the lounge and her book. She and Ralph had had talks about Marsha. She had worked through her jealousy, and knew that she and Ralph had something special. She went back to reading her book. Richard of Gloucester's problems were even more complicated that her own.

Sally was quite surprised a few days later to receive a phone call from Marsha. Marsha came straight to the point.

"Don't you think that you are holding Ralph back?" she accused.

Sally was stunned. "How do you mean?" was her reply.

"Ralph could be really successful on the lecture and TV circuit if you would only let him."

"Hang on a minute! I have never stopped him doing anything he wanted to do. But he has told me repeatedly, that he does not want to be a TV pundit. And I know that he has told you so."

"How do you know that?"

"I heard him tell you the other day."

"Hell, you were listening?"

"Not really. It was just that your voices were raised. I'm surprised that the whole neighbourhood didn't hear. You ought to know by now that Ralph will do what he wants to do. Once he has made up his mind there is no stopping him. I understand that he left you and he had his reasons then. You won't change his mind now."

"But can't you change his mind?"

"Why should I do anything to benefit you, when you have tried to break us up?"

"Because it would be good for him."

"I've told you. He knows what he wants. Why should he do what I want?"

"Because if he doesn't, I'll make his life hell. I know things about him that you don't. How would you like his colleagues to hear about them?"

"I think that says more about you than about him. I'm sure he knows a thing or two about you if you go down that road. No one will win and you will definitely lose."

Sally told Ralph about the conversation, later when he came home from the Jorvik.

"I was afraid of that," he said. "I knew she had a vicious streak. She might be able to wreck my career but would she wreck us?"

"I don't think so, my love. I've known you a long time, I'm afraid that you're stuck with me."

"That's how it should be," he said putting his arms around her. "As long as we are secure, let her do her worst."

Chapter 31

It was shortly after this that Sally had her break-through connecting Alice Atherton to William Allanson. Using both the resources of the Gisburn Archive and the websites devoted to family history, she discovered that Sir William Allanson who bought Crayke Castle in 1648 was married twice. Firstly, he married Lucy Orracke, a marriage which produced no children. Lucy must have died before 1632 because he married as his second wife Anne Tancred, at Whixley, a village situated between York and Knaresborough, in 1632. Their son Charles was born in 1633. William died in 1656 and his son Charles took over Crayke Castle and restored it. He also married twice his first wife being Frances Whorwood, the daughter of Sir Thomas Whorwood; they had a daughter, Margaret, who was born about 1655. Frances died in 1659 because he married again this time to Grace Jacques, and they had a daughter in 1661 and their son was born in 1662. Following the restoration of King Charles II in 1660, the Castle at Crayke was restored to the See of Durham in 1667. Charles died in 1676 in York. Margaret married in 1680 a man called Richard Murgatroyd one of the Wensleydale Murgatroyds. They had a daughter, Frances named after Margaret's mother who was born in 1685 and she married John Atherton of Warrington, Lancashire in 1705.

Sally deduced that Charles had found the pouch during his restoration of Crayke Castle and given it and the letter to Margaret as her inheritance, on her marriage, to keep it well away from his family. Whether either Margaret, or her husband, had known what it contained, Sally could only speculate. One way she could discover if the existence of the pouch was known at this time, was to find a will for Charles Allanson in which reference was made to it. Therefore, Sally hunted through the wills-indexes in the Gisburn without immediate success, and then through the indexes which were available online. She eventually found one in the North Yorkshire Archives in Northallerton which meant a journey to see it.

The following day she took the car and set off for Northallerton. The Archives were very helpful and before too long she had the will in front of her. With a deep breath, she looked through it. It was dated August 1676 and had a probate attached. After reading it through, she made notes of everything it said, including the reference code given to it by the Archives. Briefly, it made no direct mention of the pouch but at the end said, "Lastly, I bequeath to my daughter Margaret the relic which was found at Crayke in the hope that she will keep it safe until it is required." Was this the pouch with its revolutionary contents? Had it been opened, and the letter read? If so, why was it still being kept secret when the concealment was no longer required? Charles II was a descendant of the House of York. Edward IV's daughter, Elizabeth had married King Henry VII and her daughter, Margaret, married King James IV of Scotland, and was the grandmother of King James VI of Scotland and James II of England, from whom Charles II was descended, so an heir to the House of York actually sat on the throne. The prince who wrote the letter, if it was genuine, would have been Margaret's uncle and would surely not have quarrelled with him over the throne. By this time, the letter would have posed no threat to the crown.

However, it would appear, that the curse, that Alice Atherton believed, belonged to it was still very real and the pouch had remained with the family as a legend.

Sally now knew that Margaret Allanson who married Richard Murgatroyd had been given the pouch. Was it mentioned in any later wills? While still in Northallerton, Sally consulted the indexes as well as the websites and found that Margaret Murgatroyd had made a will when she died in 1725. Now she found that the will was in the Gisburn Archive back in York. So back to York she trekked arriving just after lunch time. As she parked the car, the first person she saw was Ralph on his way to the senior common room restaurant.

"Hey up lass," he called as he made his way towards her. "How did you get on?"

"I've had a wonderful morning," she said as she kissed him. "I found the will and there is a mention of a relic found at Crayke. It was left to Charles's daughter Margaret and now I am after her will which is here in the Gisburn."

"Have you eaten?" he asked.

"Not yet; I haven't had time."

"Come with me and tell me all about it while we have a late lunch of whatever might be available." They went into the senior common room.

Over a sandwich lunch which was all that was still going, she told him what she had found and the importance of it.

"Now I've to see Margaret's will, and if there is any mention of anything like a pouch then I think that we might be on the right lines."

"This will is here, in the Gisburn?"

"It's supposed to be. I'll let you know how I get on tonight. How are things with you?"

"I gave my presentation this morning to the department," he said.

"Oh, no," Sally replied. "I forgot all about it once I had set off. How did it go?"

"They seemed to like it. In fact, a couple of them were quite enthusiastic and raring to go, so now I have to get in touch with Marsha to find an agent, and a TV company, and the rest of it. I never thought that I would be doing this," he said. "Do you mind me getting in touch with her?"

"No. I suppose that we could have her over for dinner again, to see if she behaves herself. Sometimes it is best to make friends with those who might cause problems for you."

"Let's see how we go first. I have no interest in her and she is sure to tell me that I am going about it the wrong way. So, if you and I work together on it with her and the department, then we should get it off the ground and hopefully, without any major problems."

They left the senior common room together and Sally went into the Gisburn to ask for Margaret Murgatroyd's will having looked up the Reference code in the index. After a short wait, Susan Hartley brought it to her.

"Are you working on the project?" she asked.

"Yes. I'll let you know how I get on," Sally replied. "I've had a good day so far."

She took the will and opened it. It was rather long and detailed, and the writing was unfamiliar so she had to spend some time deciphering it before she could make head or tail of it. Again, she transcribed it as she went along leaving gaps where she could not quite make out a word and then coming back to the missing word when she had got the sense of the whole. And there it was. Again, as it had been in the last entry on her father's will was a reference to the pouch.

"Lastly, I leave to my daughter the wife of John Atherton now of Helmsley the relic given to me by my father for safety which has been kept close by me and trust that she will do the same."

There, that was the link that Sally had been looking for. Now all she had to do was find out how the pouch got to Crayke in the first place.

Chapter 32

One evening early in November when Sally got home, she found that she was first. Ralph must be still at the university. She had begun preparations for the evening meal when she heard the door open and close downstairs and knew that Ralph was home. She heard the scuffle in the hall as he brought his bicycle in, and then his feet on the stairs as he climbed to the kitchen.

"How do, love?" he said as he came through the door.

Sally looked at him.

"What's wrong?" she said, he looked worn out.

"As I was leaving Marsha rang me back.," he replied. "I had tried her earlier when she was out, and she had rung me back. She was over the moon that I had at last come around to her way of thinking about a TV career. She went on and on about how marvellous it would be for us both, that mean's her and me, having joint careers. It looks as though she thinks that I am going to go back to her. It was quite exhausting."

"I was afraid that something like that might happen when you approached her but if the department needs the publicity, then I suppose it must be done."

"Looks like it, I'm afraid."

"If you are absolutely sure that it's in the department's best interests then I am with you," Sally said. "I think that the best thing we can do is present her with a united front and show her that she doesn't stand a chance."

"Until just now, as I was cycling back," he said. "I suddenly realised that this was home, and you were here and you were home, so she had no chance of breaking us up. I love you." He put his arms around her and held her tight. This was his world. Sally put down the pan she had been holding and returned his hug.

"You know," she said, "I often thought before we met what the man I married would be like, that is if I ever met anyone who would want to marry me, and you are more that I could ever have imagined. As far as I'm concerned, we are a team and we face all our problems together and we will get the better of them one way or another." They stood for a while just being comforted by each other's presence.

"Now tell me how the day went before you contacted Marsha." While he was talking Sally went back to preparing the evening meal and began the process of stirring a risotto on the hob. Ralph leant again the working surface, well out of her way, as he talked.

"Well, it was all going swimmingly. Jeremy like my proposal and the rest of the department did too, that is, as long as they did not have to appear on camera, so I was given the go ahead to make enquiries from Marsha as to how to go about getting it filmed. There are apparently lots of educational channels that will take this kind of information which is where we were when I saw you at lunch. Then I put a call in to Marsha, and it went downhill from there. However, I'm sure, with your help, we can get it back on track."

"Well, you know I will do all I can." By this time, the meal was cooked, and they sat at the dining table to eat. When they had finished, they put the crockery into the dishwasher before going into the lounge with their after-dinner drinks, coffee for Ralph and drinking chocolate for Sally.

They were sitting together on the settee when Ralph asked. "How was your day? You said you were having a good day."

"Yes," replied Sally. "I have finally got proof that the pouch or a relic as it was referred to in the two wills I found, actually existed in the sixteenth and seventeenth centuries and was in the hands of the Atherton family. Alice said that her family farmed over by Helmsley and that is where they were in 1725, when Margaret Murgatroyd died. She mentions the relic in her will, in relation to her daughter Frances, who was married to John Atherton of Helmsley. I have found a chain from there down to Miss Atherton in Pickering. All I have to do now is find out how it got from Sir John Conyers and Hornby Castle to Crayke. Not much left to do then!"

"I know you did a lot in research into Sir John Conyers and his family when you were looking into Robin of Redesdale," remembered Ralph. "Did you come across anything then?"

"No. The period I was looking at then was much earlier, in the 1469–71 range. The letter in the pouch wasn't apparently written until after 1487 but before 1490, so I will have to look for any mention of it after that, as well as seeing if the Conyers family had any dealings with Crayke. So, it will be back to the Archives tomorrow."

"I had hoped to help you when this all started but I'm afraid, love, that I am going to be tied up with this TV project. But keep me posted. I would hate to discover that you had disappeared into the fifteenth century without leaving me a clue. Like Orpheus, I might have to come and find you, to get you back to this century."

"Oh, would that be too much trouble then?" asked Sally. "I rather thought that if that happened, you would want to come to find me. After all your talk of taking on Dragons on Winter Hill, I find that you can't actually face the jaws of the past. I am disillusioned."

"I walked into that, didn't I? I see that I shall have to much more careful about how I phrase things in future. Of course, I would come to rescue you. Actually, if you succeed, I might have to rescue you from an angry mob of academics who won't like you challenging their cherished version of Richard III."

"That's true. So, you had better keep your trusty sword, sharp and in good order, ready for the fray. On the other hand, if you keep teasing me about Richard III and the Princes, you might need it to defend yourself from me!"

"Do you know you have got me worried now? I thought I would never need it once I had won my fair lady and I had left it in the attic in Cleckheaton."

"Isn't that just like a man? When you want a prince charming, he's left his sword at home. What is the world coming to?" Sally kissed him.

"No," Ralph said gently pushing her away. "I do not deserve a kiss. I have let my fair lady down. I have entered the lists unarmed. Hold! Wait a mo'!" He dashed downstairs and Sally heard him rooting in the garage. *What on earth is he up to,* she thought. Minutes later, she heard him running up the stairs; he entered the living room with a flourish. In his hand was the little wooden sword he had had as a child when he had gone looking for dragons on Emley Moor.

"Behold," he exclaimed, "here is my trusty sword." He brandished it in the air. "Ready, my lady, to defend you from the wrath of countless academics on any stage. Not only that I have found my shield. We are secure."

"You're as mad as I am," Sally replied. "But I always knew that my 'Parfait gentle knight' would come through."

"I suddenly remembered that there was a box of my stuff left in the garage which I had not gone through. So had a look and there they were. Is all forgiven, my lady?" he said as he knelt before her.

"Yes, sir knight. You have regained your lady's favour."

"In that case," said the knight, "let's go to bed."

Sally laughed. "Your seduction technique leaves something to be desired."

"Eeh, lass," he replied, "I come from Yorkshire. I have no time for subtle southern ways. Are you coming?"

"I'll show you how it should be done," replied Sally. She grabbed her husband's neck and pulling his face down, she kissed him forcing her tongue between his teeth. Releasing one arm, she pulled his shirt out of the waist band of his trousers and pushed her hand up his back caressing him passionately all the time. Ralph, meantime, was stunned, she had never done anything like this before but caught up in her passion responded as only he knew how.

When he did, Sally said, "See you up there," and ran up the stairs with Ralph close behind.

Once in the bedroom, passion took over and before they knew it, they were naked, in bed, enjoying each other as they had not done since the early days of their relationship. Sally took charge and initiated sex on top which made Ralph her slave. Then it was Ralph's turn. Turn and about they went until they fell fast asleep, satiated, in each other's arms. Content this was what they hoped marriage would be but somehow other things got in the way.

Chapter 33

Over the next few days, Sally made a determined effort to sort out the descendants of Sir John Conyers. Using an online website, she found that, because his son had died at the Battle of Edgecote in 1469 his heir, was his grandson William. Before 1469, Sir John had been a supporter of Richard Neville, Earl of Warwick, and had therefore given him his support during his quarrel with Edward IV. This uprising has been called the Yorkshire Rebellion. *When did Yorkshire, not rise in rebellion?* Sally thought. As usual, this started out over taxation. One semi-mythical figure who had dominated the rebellion was Robin of Redesdale. Rededale itself is situated in Northumberland above Otterburn, and the use of the name would have given the impression that the rebellion had broader roots than just being Yorkshire based. However, there was ample evidence that Robin of Redesdale, was either Sir John Conyers, or his son, also John Conyers, who played the part. There was another faction to the rebellion whose leader was known as Robin of Holderness but he has been identified as belonging to a different family.

Following the death of Warwick at the Battle of Barnet, and the restoration of King Edward IV, the Neville estates of Middleham, in particular, were granted to Edward's brother, Richard Duke of Gloucester. Sir John Conyers changed his allegiance to support his new overlord and served him faithfully until the Battle of Bosworth in 1485. Whether this change of allegiance was also brought about, by the visit that Richard had made to Hornby Castle in 1469, which would have given Conyers ample opportunity to assess the man, Sally could not be sure.

After the death of Edward IV, Sir John has been at the coronation of King Richard and when Richard was defeated at Bosworth Henry VII dismissed him from his posts. Sir John played no part in the Lambert Simnel affair and retained his estates, so it appeared to Sally that Richard of Shrewsbury or York, could have written to Sir John in the months following the Battle of Stoke Field in 1487.

Sally's next question was, "What could have happened to the letter after Sir John's death in 1490?"

Sir John's heir, his grandson William, was born in 1468 shortly before his father died, and was a relatively young man when he inherited from his grandfather. William married twice, firstly to Mary, daughter of Lord Scrope of Bolton in Wensleydale (The Scropes of Bolton had joined in the Lambert Simnel affair on the Simnel side), and secondly to Anne Neville, daughter of Sir Ralph Neville, 3rd Earl of Westmorland. William died in 1524 and his son Christopher, succeeded him died in 1538. Christopher, in his turn, had one son, John who became 3rd Baron Conyers and when he died in 1557, he left four daughters and no son. It was the son of his eldest daughter, Elizabeth who married Thomas Darcy. Her son, called Conyers Darcy eventually inherited the title and became 4th Baron Conyers in about 1641. So, Sally pondered as to whether it was on the death of William in 1524 or John in 1557 when the letter and pouch were deposited at Crayke?

Sally could see that there was a problem as 1557 was after Henry VIII's break with Rome, when the power of the church had been taken over by the King. King Henry was someone who would have been very interested in the contents of the letter if he had known about it. Following his father's example, he began to systematically remove all the possible Plantagenet claimants to the throne even to the extent of executing the 68-year-old Margaret, Countess of Salisbury in May 1541. So once the break with Rome had occurred it would have been expedient to put the letter in a place of safety in the hands of the church at Crayke.

If John Conyers, the 3rd Baron who had inherited in 1538 and, having only daughters at this point, had decided to give the pouch and letter to the Diocese of Durham would he have even told his daughters what he planned to do? If it was deposited at this point in history, it would lie undetected for the next hundred years? At which time, the paranoid Tudors had passed away and the Stuarts had taken the throne. In that time, the letter and pouch would be forgotten. Richard of Shrewsbury would be dead by then. If he had married, had an heir then somewhere in Europe there could be a living claimant to the throne.

Sally now realised that she would have to trawl through all the archives to see if there was reference to any document which tied the Conyers family to Crayke, and with a wider trawl through any archive with documents from the period.

When Sally explained this to Ralph, she saw his face fall. He realised, as she had, the amount of material which would have to be gone through. Obviously, some of the searching could be done on the internet but if it also involved visiting the archives than that would take up precious time that they hoped to save for themselves.

Sally now began the hunt. She did it from home and one by one eliminated all the archives she could think of. Their catalogues did not give any clue as the whereabouts of any Conyers papers from any period, let alone the period she particularly wanted. She would have to go back to Stanley Fisher and tell him that she had failed in her second task.

Chapter 34

On Wednesday morning, Sally went into the Gisburn Archives and straight to Dr Fisher's office.

"I'm sorry," she said. "I've looked at all the likely archives, and some less likely ones without any real success. I am horribly afraid that we are not going to find the corroborative detail that we need to confirm the deposit of the letter."

"Well, that is a great pity," Dr Fisher replied. "But I have got one suggestion for you. Arthur Cliff, of the History Department, is doing some research on the descendants of the Conyers family from the Reformation, to the civil war period, I'm not sure which. He may be able to help. It would be a good idea if you go and have a word with him."

"Is that a very good idea?" questioned Sally. "I know that history does not get on with Anglo-Saxon at the moment, and I don't want to cause Ralph any problems."

"Just go and see him. Tell him what you want. I think he might help if he can."

Sally left the comfort of the Gisburn Archive and went to find the History Faculty building. On reaching it, she enquired of the first person she met for the location of Arthur Cliff's room, which turned out to be on the second floor. She approached it rather tentatively and knocked. On being invited in, she entered.

Arthur Cliff was a man of about Sally's age (mid-30s), short with blonde hair in a shaggy mane and a scowl on his otherwise pleasant face.

"Who the devil, are you?" he asked. "I was expecting a student."

"I'm Sally Armstrong, and Dr Fisher of the Gisburn, has suggested that I come to see if you can help me with a project I'm working on."

"Well, I can give you a few minutes until my student turns up but they are already late and may not come. Student's these days." Then he said, "Armstrong! Armstrong! Now where have I heard that name before?" He pondered for a moment and then added, "That's it, there's a man of that name, who's an ass."

"I beg your pardon?" said Sally. "How do you mean he's an ass?"

"Sorry, I don't mean that he is an ass just that he is in ASS, the Anglo-Saxon Studies Department."

"Yes, that is correct. Dr Armstrong is in the Anglo-Saxon Studies Department, and before you decide to say something else derogatory, I should tell that he is my husband."

"Ouch!" exclaimed Arthur Cliff.

"So, before we go any further, do you think that we can start again?"

He nodded in an embarrassed way.

"Right," said Sally. "Good morning. I am Sally Armstrong and I have been sent by Dr Fisher of the Gisburn to ask you if you can help."

"Good," said Mr Cliff. "How can I be of assistance?"

"I am trying to locate some information about the Conyers family from the late fifteenth and early sixteenth centuries. I've looked at the archive indexes and there doesn't seem to be very much from that period. For some reason, Dr Fisher thought you might be able to help."

"I'm doing my Ph.D. thesis on the 3rd Baron Conyers 1524–1557 and one of his descendants has very kindly given me a file of information, which they were still holding in private hands. I keep it in the Gisburn for safety and security, and among the items included, I found a bundle of material from his father Christopher's time and mentioned it to Stanley. What is your interest in it?"

"I had been doing some grunt work in the Gisburn to help the local Family History Societies, when an item was given to the Archive. It dates from the later fifteenth century and was apparently found in Crayke Castle in the Civil War Period. I am trying to find out how it got there."

"How do the Conyers family come into it?"

"It appears that the item was at one time in the Conyers' hands. I'm afraid the details are still top secret at the moment. What I am looking for is anything that looks as though it could be a record of a deposit from any member of the Conyers family."

"As far as I'm concerned, you can have a look at that little bundle. I did have a look at the contents but when I realised it was of no use to me, I just put it back. But you will have to contact the owner to see if they have any objection to you looking at it. If the answer to your puzzle is in there, then I presume it, could have major implications."

"That's true," said Sally and thought *You don't know how major*, before adding, "Please can you give me details of the owner?"

"No, can do. Until I have finished my thesis and it's been accepted, they want to remain anonymous. If it ever gets published, then they realise that their anonymity will have to be revealed, and they might decide to deposit the whole file in the Gisburn Archive."

"Will you get in touch with them then for me?" asked Sally. "Obviously, the same caveat on publication would apply to any document found. But if a document exists, it will solve several major historical conundrums."

"As bad as that! I'll see what I can do. If it is of such historical importance, it might not do my own career any harm to be associated with it."

"Thank you very much," said Sally. "You can contact me through Dr Fisher at the Gisburn, or through Ralph in ASS," she continued with a twinkle.

"I'll get in touch later today and let you know what's possible."

"Many thanks," said Sally, and shaking Mr Cliff's hand, she left his office.

Chapter 35

Morning lectures were over, and it was just after lunchtime when Sally got home and found Ralph was there already, working on the garden. He had already eaten, so Sally made herself a sandwich. Ralph was determined, that next year, they would be able to sit out and enjoy all their hard work. Now he was doing some late tidying ready for the winter. Anything to take his mind off the prospect of making television programmes.

"You'll never guess who I've been talking to today?" said Sally.

"Go on," was the reply.

"Someone who called you an ass."

"Oh! Someone in the history faculty then."

"That's right. Mind you I put him right. It was Arthur Cliff. Stanley Fisher sent me to see him. He thought that he might be able to help with the project."

"And did he?"

"Well, he's going to get back to me on that. But at the moment, it sounds hopeful. He might give you a message for me. What is the problem there?"

"It's this problem with the future of Anglo-Saxon Studies. The History faculty want to take over and submerge AS in its remit. Us AS bods want to retain out independence. As you know, the university was founded to support Anglo-Saxon, so that is why this idea of some TV programmes is so attractive to the AS mob. It would be good publicity for us and for the university. On the other hand, History would benefit as well. Unfortunately, they don't see it like that and are trying to make a takeover grab."

"That's a pity because surely if you all work together you'll all benefit."

"That's what I keep telling them. Can we change the subject? It's beginning to get me down."

Sally could see this on Ralph's face and went in to make a reviving cup of tea.

Later that afternoon, Sally got a message to ring Arthur Cliff and his response when she finally tracked him down was encouraging.

"I've been in touch with the owner of the document file, and she is willing to meet you to discuss your project. She lives near Leeds, and this is her number. Have you got pen and paper, she's called, Mrs Osborne." Sally reached for a pen and paper and took down the number.

The following day, Sally rang the number and Mrs Osborne answered.

"Come and see me," she said when Sally told her who she was. She gave her an address in Garforth. "I should like to look you in the eye while we talk."

They made arrangements to meet the following Wednesday afternoon.

Mrs Osborne's house was more imposing than Sally had expected. It was double fronted and detached with a large garden at the front. *Who lives in a house like this?* she thought.

However, Mrs Osborne was most welcoming when Sally arrived on her doorstep.

"Come in," she said as she showed Sally into the very pleasant lounge which faced the rear garden and got all the sun in the morning.

"Now then," she continued, "I understand from Arthur, that you would like to look at the documents I have lent him?"

"Well," Sally began and continued, "I should like to look at some of them and see what they consist of. I am looking for something quite specific, if it exists at all. I have found no trace of anything like it up to now. I must admit it is a bit like looking for a needle in a haystack. I was referred to Mr Cliff by Dr Fisher of the Gisburn Archive because the archive is looking after your documents while Mr Cliff is using them. They are quite safe there, and I have not been allowed to even see the box. Dr Fisher knew that there was a third party but does not know your name."

"I had better tell you the story," began Mrs Osborne. "I was approached by Arthur, who by the way, is a distant relation of mine because I was given a box of papers when my aunt died. She was, herself, a distant member of the Vavasour family of Hazelwood Castle, and had inherited the papers when her uncle died many years ago. Arthur found out about them through the family grapevine, and as he was interested in the 3rd Baron Conyers, and as some of the papers seem to relate to him, I thought that they might help him with his research. We are all descended from Baron Conyers in some way. Now, I understand that there was some earlier material in the box, which is what I think you are interested in. Is that the case?"

"The Gisburn Archive has been given a document which, if it is authentic, has a great deal of historical significance," Sally began. "Unfortunately, I can't tell you what it is at the moment. What I'm doing is trying to trace its provenance, and any document that can help with that would be of great value. Not necessarily in monetary terms but historically."

"Go on," Mrs Osborne was intrigued.

"I am looking to see if there is any evidence, direct evidence that is, that the document was deposited by a member of the Conyers family at either Crayke Castle, or with the Diocese of Durham, at any time between 1490 and 1640," Sally explained. "You are right. I understand from Mr Cliff, that there is a bundle of papers from that earlier period in the file you have lent him. I was hoping that you would allow me to have access to them at this stage, just to see if there is anything that would be helpful."

"Would my involvement in this need to come out?"

"Only if there is such a document and only then if you wanted the fact known. Your family connection would be enough to validate the authenticity of the document in the bundle, and that in turn, would validate the document I am researching," reassured Sally.

"I only let Arthur have the file because of his interest in our family history," said Mrs Osborne rather wistfully. "If I had known it was going to cause all this fuss, I would never have agreed."

"I am sorry to cause you any problems," apologised Sally. "And I would not ask if there was any other way but I'm afraid I am running out of options. Sometimes the most important non-governmental documents are still held in private hands, as the official copy has been lost over time, and it looks as though this may be one of those occasions."

"Well, thank you for your explanation. I think what I should like to suggest is that you look at the bundle and find out what it contains. If there is nothing there, then nothing has been lost. If you find what you are looking for, come back to me and I'll think again."

"That is most kind," said Sally. She left Garforth with the knowledge that there was still something she could do before all doors were closed. In an optimistic frame of mind, she drove back to York, having rung Dr Fisher to tell him she would come into the Gisburn in the morning.

Chapter 36

When Sally entered Dr Fisher's office the next morning, she was surprised to find Arthur Cliff there already.

"Arthur has just come to tell me that Mrs Osborne, his anonymous benefactor, has rung him to say that you can look at the file he has borrowed," Dr Fisher said. "I understand that there are various provisos which you will tell me about."

"Yes," replied Sally. "Mrs Osborne has kindly agreed that I can look at the documents and only if they are of any use then we will then take it further. Have you told Mr Cliff what this is all about?"

"No. Not yet. I thought I would wait for you, as you have been so closely connected with it."

"In that case," Sally said, "I think that we should keep it a secret a little while longer. Not that I don't trust the history faculty but I don't trust historians to keep a secret. Word has a tendency to get out." Sally looked at Mr Cliff and gave him a wink.

"Hang on a minute," said Arthur Cliff. "I don't like the sound of this."

"Well, if you will be rude about Anglo-Saxons, then I shall be rude about historians."

"Hey up! We're all historians, you know?" Arthur Cliff was getting cross.

Good, thought Sally, *That'll larn him.*

"Now, now," said Dr Fisher, "let's not let departmental rivalry spoil a good thing. Sally, Arthur here has brought the bundle of papers. If you would like to go through them here while he waits, there can be no conflict."

"Sounds good to me," Sally said. She took the bundle to a reading desk in the main reading room and Mr Cliff came and sat on an adjacent seat. She carefully separated the items, and read the rubric heading on each one. In the middle of the bundle was a single sheet of paper headed 'Crayke'. Her heart rose.

"This looks promising," she said. She carefully unfolded the sheet and spread it out and held it by its corner. She left it on the table and went across and got four stones from the weighting basket and put one on each corner to hold it flat as she read. Yes. This was what she had been looking for.

"To Lord Counyers litters tuis acceptis et saccs salvus sospes ad infinitum ad Crayke. Mdxxix."

"Eureka," said Sally, "look at this."

"It just looks like a receipt for something," said Arthur.

"That's just what it is. I'm going to photograph it if you don't mind, and then show it to Dr Fisher." Before Arthur could get a word in, that is just what she did, with Arthur trailing along behind her.

Dr Fisher sat back in his chair when she told him what she had found and showed him the photograph. He came out of his office and looked at the document spread out on the table. It was then carefully replaced in the bundle, which was then put back in the file.

"Well, that's that then," he said. "We had better tell Miss Atherton."

"Now, can you tell me what this all about?" asked Arthur.

"Not just yet. But as soon as all the relevant people have been told, you will be the next to know. Please say nothing to anyone until then," begged Dr Fisher.

"My lips are sealed," Arthur said. He was still in the dark but realised if he was discrete, he could be in at the beginning of something big.

"Are you really opposed to the Anglo-Saxons?" asked Sally, as they left the Gisburn.

"No not really," replied Arthur Cliff. "I know some of my colleagues pretend that AS is all a form of myth and legend but we, as a people, had to originate from somewhere. It's just a pity that because it has its own language, it makes it difficult for the students who, of course, want everything on a plate these days."

"But you must have started somewhere if you are looking at the Barons Conyers."

"It just seemed to come to me. My ancestors were Yorkshire gentry/nobility, and I got curious about them. Then, of course, there was the Reformation, and I wondered how they coped with the changes, which is how I got to the 3rd Baron, who if the date on that document is not wrong, could be the one I am looking at. I am now, more than interested in what this is all about."

"I got involved because of my interest in the last Plantagenets," said Sally discretely.

"Are you an historian as well?" he asked.

"No. I'm only an amateur but I am a librarian when I am at it. There are no jobs going these days, so I am filling in time helping with projects where I can."

"Look," he said, "have you time to come and have lunch in the senior common room and we can talk some more?"

"If Ralph is there, perhaps we can join him," said Sally. "I should like you to meet him properly, if you don't mind. I think it would be good if this antagonism within your department is put to bed, don't you?"

They went across to the SCR and found Ralph having a solitary sandwich and they joined him.

Chapter 37

The academic term was ending and there were only a few academic staff present. Most of the students had gone home for Christmas so it was a good time to talk. Ralph moved his papers to make room for them on his table.

"What's been going on," he said.

"Hi Ralph," said Arthur Cliff.

"Oh! Ralph," said Sally. "I didn't know whether you knew Mr Cliff. He has been very helpful with the project I've been working on."

"You mean…Oh! I shouldn't say anything should I?"

"That's right," said Sally. "You remember you swore an oath of secrecy."

"So, I did. Ooops. Doesn't Arthur know about it then?"

"That's right. And the less said about it the better."

"Yes, I do know who Arthur is," replied Ralph. "I have seen you around, of course, but you weren't a fan of Anglo-Saxon Studies."

"That's not strictly true," said Arthur. "I just think that there has been too much emphasis on it in the past, and history has a better chance of surviving. Let's face it we are all part of history. Why should Anglo-Saxon get a bigger share than, say, my period? The Civil War came to Yorkshire, just as much as the Anglo-Saxons did."

"Fair point," said Ralph. "However, if you know the history of the university, you know that it was founded to preserve our Anglo-Saxon heritage. Therefore, we are about to raise the profile of the subject."

"How?"

"Publicity. A friend of mine," Ralph replied looking anxiously at Sally, "is into TV broadcasts and is interested in promoting Anglo-Saxon as a new subject to her production company."

"Who's that?"

"Marsha Hamilton."

"You know her? Wow. I've been trying to meet her as I teach her period, but without success. Do you think you could arrange for me to meet her?" Arthur was gushing, obviously smitten.

"Well, I could," mused Ralph, not really relishing the prospect of having more contact with Marsha. "But she seems to have the Civil War Period tied up for herself. So, I don't know how much help I can be."

"I would just like to meet her," said Arthur. "I've been a big fan. Actually, she is the reason I got into history in the first place."

"Don't tell her that." Ralph laughed. "She won't thank you for giving away how long she's been on the box."

"Will do." Arthur joined the laughter. "But thanks anyway."

"It looks as though we may have to arrange another dinner party," said Sally. "If we can get a date fixed, I'll get in touch. I owe you at least that much for all the help you've been. Have you got a partner?"

"Yes, I have a wife, who unfortunately, does not share my enthusiasm for history. She is a nurse but she loves dinner parties."

"I'll get in touch then, or send a message via Ralph," said Sally. "At least I know where you reside, room 302 on the second floor."

"It's been very interesting meeting you in a less stressful situation," said Arthur to Ralph, as he got up to leave. "I hope it won't be too long before I find out what all this has been about." He left them together.

"Gosh," said Ralph. "What has happened?"

"I'll tell you when we get home," said Sally, "but it is all good."

"I had better get off to my next meeting. Probably the one Arthur has just gone off to. I'll see you tonight. I want all the details."

When Ralph got home, he found Sally in his study making notes on sheets of paper.

"That's a bit old hat, isn't it?" he said.

"Yes, my love, but I dare not put anything on a computer that can be hacked."

"As bad as that?"

"Yes. I am writing a report for Stanley Fisher, on what I have done and what I've found out," said Sally, "but I have had a brilliant idea, I think Arthur should write the explosive paper that's going to reveal all."

"Why him? You've done all the work."

"Because his family history is linked to the document, and it would look good coming from him as an historian, and it would not do the department or the university any harm, if he was the one to break the news," explained Sally.

"So, what has happened?" asked Ralph.

"There is a receipt for the pouch being at Crayke, among the documents that Arthur was working on. He had not given it much thought, even though it dated from the 3rd Baron Conyers whom he was researching. It was among a batch of family papers. He is a descendant of the Conyers, among others. The papers had been handed down through the family to Mary Osborne who I went to see yesterday. She was willing for me to have a look at them and there it was…"

"So, what happens now?"

"We tell Alice Atherton about it. Then Mrs Osborne and in the meantime, I write a report which is what I was doing when you came home."

"Can we have dinner, and I will tell you all about my day?" said Ralph.

Over the meal, Ralph told Sally about the meeting he had been to. "Arthur had also been there, and one of the items on the agenda, had been the proposed television series about the Anglo Saxons. The History faculty, in general, were opposed in that it limited the scope of the department but for once Arthur came in on the Anglo-Saxon side. He had repeated what he said over lunch, that we are all part of history, and that we should all have an equal chance for development."

"That must be because I jumped on him when he called you asses. Or something like that," said Sally. "The History Faculty seems to have become very territorial."

"When did he call us asses?"

"The other day when I met him, I told you about it."

"So, you did. Isn't amazing how spending such a short time with someone, can change their perspective?"

"Sure is, love," said Sally. "But you did all the hard work over lunch. So, is everybody in favour of the project now?"

"Looks like it." Ralph was relieved. "I may not be the main presenter as Marsha thought I ought to be, but I will probably be in there somewhere being very dramatic over Anglo-Saxon Poetry of which there is a fair amount."

"I'm glad it's all working out for you. I know how worried you've been over the future of the department."

"I think I'd better go and work of my surplus energy in the garden," Ralph said as they stacked the dishwasher.

"Is there anything for you to do? It's December," asked Sally.

"To be honest, not a lot but I find being outside refreshes the parts being inside doesn't reach. Thought I might go and tidy the shed."

"I'll get back to my report then," said Sally, she knew what tidying the shed meant. A new cask of mead had just arrived.

For the coming season, Sally was surprised to find that she was included in the Archives Christmas party and was encouraged to bring Ralph along. At the same time, Ralph was encouraged to bring Sally to the Anglo-Saxon Christmas bash and two very good evenings were had by all. Sally enjoyed meeting her husband's colleagues now that the thorny question of the future of Anglo-Saxon Studies had been settled. Filming was to start in the New Year so there was a good deal of banter about who was going to be the star.

Chapter 38

It was not until after Christmas that Sally was able to take the first draft of her report into the Gisburn. When she did, she found Dr Fisher on the telephone. She waited outside his office until he had finished and then went in.

"Here is the first draft of my report, on the pouch and letter," said Sally as she handed it to him.

"Many thanks, for all you've done," replied Dr Fisher. "I've just been on the phone to Miss Atherton and arranged to go and see her later next week. She has some appointments and when she gets them sorted, she's going to let me know when."

"I have really enjoyed this experience," said Sally. "If you have any more projects, please let me know."

"Do you have any expenses?"

"Not really. Just a couple of car trips to Pickering and Garforth, both of which I enjoyed, so no. The fee we agreed for the work will cover them."

"I'll put the request through, if you will fill out this claim form," he said as he handed it to her.

"What is going to happen to the publication?" Sally asked; she really wanted to know.

"I will have to discuss it with the board, as you know it is a major document and the publicity must be handled carefully."

"My report details all the steps I took to reach my conclusions," said Sally, "so that they can be independently verified, if you think that is what is needed. Knowing how the academic world has attacked Richard III over the disappearance of the Princes they are not going to take this news without strict examination."

"I'm aware of that but if we can get the History Faculty on board with this then there shouldn't be a problem from this end."

"I had a thought about that. I know that I am only an amateur and realise that professional input is vital. I was going to suggest that Arthur Cliff should be involved in that. He is related to nearly all the people in the story. The Conyers, the Scropes, the Vavasours etc. And he is working on his Ph.D. on Yorkshire Gentry during the Reformation, which ties in with the deposit of the pouch and letter, at Crayke."

"That is a good thought. Now you have got your teeth into serious historical research, are you going to be able to go back to family history and the wills?"

"I don't know. I rather think I would like to write my thoughts on the implications of what we have found. That should keep me busy for a bit. I won't publish anything until the information is released. The secret is safe with me. Ralph knows, of course, but he has own problems at the moment."

"Do keep in touch, and if anything else comes along, I'll let you know," said Dr Fisher. "Actually I wanted to thank you for the professional way you have approached this, and I would like your name to be associated with the publication."

"As in, 'also Sally Armstrong'."

"Something like that." He then added, "I'll let you know when we are going to visit Alice. I think you should come with us."

"I still have copies of her family history material, so I should find out if she wants it back."

"See you next week if not before then." Dr Fisher shook Sally's hand and as she left his office the phone rang. He picked up the receiver and answered it and called her back, "What about Thursday, next week, 8 February?"

"Yes, that suits me," said Sally.

"9:30 set off time from here."

"It's a date."

Sally left the Gisburn and went down into York and to Monk Bar and the Richard III Experience. She paid the entrance fee and went up to the middle floor. She was alone. She stood in silence for a short while, and then said, "Knew it."

"Knew what?" asked the attendant, who had just come up the stairs.

"He didn't murder the Princes in the Tower."

"Of course not, that was Henry VII. Though, if you go to the Henry VII Experience, they'll tell you differently."

Sally looked at her watch. "I think I had better go home," she said.

That evening over dinner, Sally told Ralph about the forthcoming trip to Pickering and pondered on what, or how much, she should tell Alice Atherton.

"Enough so that she knows the importance of the document, without blinding her with too much detail," was Ralph's sage advice.

"But the significance of the document is so huge," said Sally.

"But only to historians and only those who are interested in the period," replied Ralph. "The rest of the world couldn't care tuppence."

"You're probably right but then, you aren't really interested in anything after 1066."

"True," said Ralph, "but the truth is the truth, so it does matter, and I can see that. But will it make any difference today?"

"I don't think so but it will to the medieval community."

"You mean there is one." Ralph laughed.

"Yes, of course but largely to groups like the Richard III Society."

"Ah, yes."

"But you are right," said Sally. She thought for a time, and then said, "I will keep it simple for Alice, unless she asks any questions, which of course I will answer in full. In the meantime, I will work on the implications."

"Let me know how you get on, my love," said Ralph. "You know that I tease you about Richard III and the Princes but I do want to know."

Chapter 39

Over the next few days, Sally began to take things easy. She was relaxed now; the major work on the project had been done. However, at times, she started feeling uncomfortable and queasy and wondered if she had been overdoing it. She had been involved with the project for a number of weeks now and had let her other interests slip. Shelf tidying at the library was in the past, and the rehearsals for the community group's production of *Calamity Jane* were nearing completion. The performances were only a couple of weeks away. Sally had been looking forward to it but now, thought that she had enough on her plate with reading and thinking, not forgetting writing, about the implication of the letter's discovery. She did not like letting people down but began to seriously consider dropping out of the show.

On the Wednesday evening before her visit to Alice Atherton, she gave Ralph her thoughts on the subject.

"Right," she said, "the letter proves that Richard of York survived the reign of Richard III, and that he lived on into the reign of Henry VII. We know that he went to the household of Sir Edward Brampton in Portugal, and that he then, returned to the Burgundian court. The letter says so. But what happened after that? We never actually hear of him again. The Lambert Simnel rising happened in 1487 and the letter seems to have been written after that. The author says that he only wants a quiet, possibly a secluded, life but is that what happened?"

"You keep taking about Lambert Simnel. Who was he? What was the affair?" asked Ralph.

"I'm sorry," said Sally. "I assumed that you knew all about him. Well, a claimant to the throne appeared to challenge Henry VII, in 1487. It was initially reported that he was the Earl of Warwick (Edward IV's brother, the Duke of Clarence's son), then the story changed, and he claimed to be Edward V, and then his brother Richard. Am I confusing you?"

"You are rather."

"Sorry about that. To continue. The claimant went to Ireland and was crowned king in Dublin and the Irish flocked to him. He also went to Burgundy where he was recognised as her nephew, by Margaret of Burgundy, who was sister to Edward IV. Anyway, he raised an army of in Ireland, and together with German mercenaries, who were paid for by Margaret, landed in Cumbria, and marched along Wensleydale, and down via York and Doncaster, to a place between Newark and Nottingham called East Stoke, where a battle was fought. Henry watched the battle from the top of the church tower. Lambert Simnel (The pretender) was captured, and many of his supporters were killed. Simnel confessed to the imposture and was put to work in the palace kitchens."

"That doesn't seem to be a bad outcome for him," said Ralph.

"Yes but he had confessed to being an impostor. The people who put him up to it were executed."

"Ah. But there was another claimant, wasn't there?"

"Yes, Perkin Warbeck. Now we come to the letter. Was Perkin Warbeck really Richard of York? That is the question," said Sally.

"That's making a big leap, isn't it?" said Ralph.

"It is. In the letter, he says that he wanted nothing to do with making a claim to the throne. So, if he was Richard of York, what could have happened to make him change his mind?" mused Sally. "On the other hand, if Perkin really was Richard of York why did he admit to being the son of a barge keeper in Tournai? He would have ended up on the scaffold just the same. But if Perkin Warbeck was an impostor, could he have also been in the household of Edward Brampton at the same time as Richard, and, perhaps, had a superficial resemblance to him, and even sometimes pretended to be him? You know what lads are like, playing games. Maybe someone saw him do this, and thought, *there's an idea*?"

"Mmm. You're really letting your imagination take over, love."

"Yes, I know. But what if that is the case? Richard of York, having seen what happened to his countrymen at the Battle of Stoke Field and the aftermath, would probably realise that any attempt to retake the throne would be doomed to failure and he would therefore have nothing to do with it."

"You mean leaving all the glory to Perkin?"

"Well, Perkin went to Scotland and did very well there, marrying Lady Katherine Douglas and having children who were called Perkins. Of course, the Scots were always trying to cause trouble in England. It was just unfortunate, that the English did not rise to support him in the same way they had for Lambert. But ten years after Stoke, times had changed."

"I thought you said that Perkin confessed to being the son of a barge keeper. Would a Plantagenet have done that?"

"Highly unlikely, I would have thought."

"So, you think that Perkin Warbeck was really a fraud?"

"Yes but that still doesn't answer the question of what happened to Richard later in his life. Maybe he went to Italy, to Rome perhaps, made himself known to the Pope and requested his protection to enable him live quietly in Italy. Perhaps he married, and had a family, and somewhere in Italy there is a young man who is the last Plantagenet claimant to the throne of England."

"You mean the Queen's claim to the throne is in question?"

"I don't really think so. Henry VII won the throne in battle at the Battle of Bosworth. I don't think that she would have to give it up easily."

"If he went to Rome and the Pope knew, do you think that his existence or that of his descendants influenced the Pope's thinking on the granting of Henry VIII's divorce from Katherine of Aragon?"

"I think that it's your turn to enter the realms of fantasy now," said Sally. "That had more to do with the power of Spain, and the gold found in the New World, than anything else. But that's only my opinion."

"But didn't someone confess to murdering the boys on Richard's orders?"

"Yes but that was James Tyrell when he was being tried for treason in 1502, long after the event. Actually, the only reference to this murder is in Sir Thomas More's life of Richard III. No copy of the confession has been found. I think that he never confessed but suited Henry to announce such a confession existed in order to put the blame for the deaths on someone, and who better than Richard III."

"So, the letter is genuine."

"Yes. The authenticity is proved. The mystery is solved."

Chapter 40

On 8th February, Sally arrived at the Gisburn Archive ready for her trip to Pickering. She had brought her copies of all the information the Alice Atherton had given her. She looked in the search room and saw her old workstation where she had spent so many happy hours typing up will witnesses and beneficiaries. *Will I ever go back to it?* She thought. She had enjoyed the work but the project of the pouch and letter was really the sort of thing that she wanted to do.

I'll have to talk to Ralph about it, she thought, *Maybe, I could do a higher degree. I wish I did not feel so peculiar in the mornings. I think the stress of the last few weeks must really be getting to me.*

Dr Fisher arrived and together they went down to the car. Susan Hartley, who had gone on the first journey, also accompanied them to make notes.

Miss Atherton, as usual, was very welcoming and soon they were sitting in her front room with its view of the church.

"I gather you have found something out?" she said after the initial pleasantries had been gone through, and tea and coffee had appeared.

"Yes, we have," said Dr Fisher. "Sally did most of the work, so she is going to bring you up to date."

"Well, as you know," Sally began, "I borrowed all your family history material that you cousin had produced. If you would like it back, I have brought it with me today. From that, and I have checked and confirmed his findings, we have learned that the pouch and the letter came from Crayke Castle, where they were found by Charles Allanson in about 1642."

"We always believed that that was where they came from," said Miss Atherton.

"It is always good to have a family tradition confirmed," said Sally. "But the letter was addressed to Sir John Conyers who died in 1490, and so we were left with the question as to how it got from him at Hornby, to Crayke. That was a more difficult question. The archives, I'm afraid were not very helpful. But due to the great good fortune of serendipity, we have traced a reference to the items in a bundle of documents which are currently in private hands. The reference was in the form of a receipt for the items being deposited at Crayke in about 1558 by the then Baron Conyers."

"So, we are now in a position to tell you that your donation to the Gisburn Archive is one of the most significant finds of the present century," Dr Fisher continued. "It is a letter written by Richard Of York, the younger son of King Edward IV. It proves that King Richard III did not murder the Princes in the Tower, as is told in popular legend. This fact, together with the recent discovery of the King's body in Leicester last September, will result in the re-writing of the history of the period. Thank you so very much for giving the Archive a place in its discovery." Dr Fisher could be a little pompous on occasion.

"You mean that tatty old thing, which has been knocking around for years, is that important." Miss Atherton was startled.

"Oh yes, never judge a book by its cover."

"Well, I never." Alice thought for a few moments and then said, "My dad was always very careful of it. I don't think he knew what it was, he never opened it but somehow, he had the feeling that we should take real good care of it. That's why I thought that you should have it when I had no one to leave it to. I'm sure he would be really pleased about that."

At that moment, Sally realised that she was going to be sick and made a dive for the bathroom.

After she returned and was sitting down again, she asked if Alice had any more questions.

"Well, if Richard III didn't murder the Princes in the Tower, why does everybody say that he did?" Alice asked.

"A very good question," answered Sally. "That is because Sir Thomas More, in his history of Richard III, said that Sir James Tyrell confessed to murdering them on King Richard's orders way back in 1485. That was, of course, when Tyrell was being tried for treason in 1502."

"So, you really are re-writing the history books," said Alice.

"We are going to put on a display of the artefacts, when we publish the results of all this research," explained Dr Fisher, "and you will, of course, be invited to attend, as will the lady who owns the receipt for the items."

"She won't be asking for them back, will she?" asked Alice.

"I doubt it," said Dr Fisher. "In fact, it is more than likely that she will donate the receipt to the Archive as well."

Sally was surprised at that, as nothing had been mentioned about Mrs Osborne.

"Thank you very much, Miss Atherton, for everything you have done for the Gisburn Archives. We will be in touch, and like all depositors you will be able to have a look at them whenever you want," said Dr Fisher, as they took their leave and drove back to the Jorvik University and the Archive.

"How are you feeling?" asked Susan Hartley, when they were safely on the journey. "You went a bit green there, for a bit."

"I have been feeling a bit queasy during the last few days. I'd better go to the chemist on the way home."

"Good idea. I should get a test if I were you." Susan smiled.

As soon as they reached York, Sally ran to her car and drove to the nearest shopping outlet, where she went into the chemist's and asked for a pregnancy testing kit. She was beginning to suspect what was going on. After purchasing what she wanted, she went into a nearby café, and, suddenly feeling a craving, ordered a bacon butty.

After eating her butty, Sally felt a bit like her old self and so had a wander around the shopping complex. Normally, she hated shopping so this was something she would not normally do. She saw some nice clothes and thought she would treat herself as she did not know when she would do this again. She bought herself a new dress, which she knew that if what she thought was true, she might not be able to wear it for a while. She did have a momentary thought that it might be right for the reception if she could still get into it. But comforting herself with the knowledge that it was not certain that she was pregnant, she finally went back to the car and drove home.

Chapter 41

On the way home, her mind was whirring. What if she was pregnant? What would Ralph think? They had talked about having a family. But that was abstract but now it could be real. Would he really want a child, someone to disrupt his life? They had never talked about the practical implications of parenthood, only about the idea in general, as something for the future. Then, she realised that Ralph's was not the only life which would be upset, hers would be as well. Then she remembered Ralph's 'can do' attitude. If they worked together as they had done up to now, they could do anything they put their minds to. She knew he would support her.

She had started making dinner when Ralph came in. He had not been to another meeting but had brought his gym kit in with him which he put in the washing machine.

"Have you had a good workout?" she asked.

"Yes, thanks love," he replied. "I thought I had better get into shape if I am going on the television. The climbing wall keeps me calm. When I'm up high, all my problems seem to fall into place, and I get perspective on them."

"That's good. Shall I tell you about my day?"

"Yes, love. Oh, I forgot. You were going to Pickering. How did you get on?"

"Fine, Miss Atherton was a sweetie as usual. She is just glad that the bit of 'old tat' which her father had treasured, has turned out to be of significance, and will be valued for all time. Also, I learned that here is going to be an event to put all the items on show to the world, and a book to go with it."

"I hope you are writing the book, after all the time and effort you have put into the project."

"Nothing was said about that. However, I might have to postpone anything major for a while."

"Why's that, love?"

"I think I might be pregnant."

"What!" Ralph exclaimed.

"I have been feeling a bit funny over the last few days, and I was sick while we were at Pickering, much to my embarrassment. Susan suggested I should get a pregnancy test."

"Well, have you tried it?"

"Not yet I was waiting for you. I wanted to try it when you were here, seeing that you were in at the beginning so to speak."

"Do you want to take it now?" he asked.

"Yes, if you are ready for the answer."

Ralph opened the packet and looked at the instructions.

"Hey, up," he said. "Apparently, the most accurate results are obtained if the test is taken in the morning."

"You mean we have to wait until tomorrow to find out for sure?"

"Looks like it."

"Thump," said Sally. "I have got myself all wound up, and now I have to wait. Will you be with me when I take it?"

"Sure thing, my love. I'm in on this too."

Sally woke in the early hours of the morning and lay for a while wondering why she had awakened? She had mostly slept all night since she had married Ralph. As she emerged from her slumber, she remembered that she might be pregnant. Ralph seemed pleased but was she? They had talked about having a family and she had stopped taking the pill so the odds were that sooner or later she would become pregnant. Now they would soon find out and the awful significance hit her. Would she make a good mother? She had enjoyed looking after her nephew and niece, James and Jen, when they were young, and she loved playing with them, but looking after a baby was not the same thing at all. Now Mags was in Cyprus, she was not going to be on hand to give help and advice. She was on her own. She did not know what Ralph knew about looking after babies, although he also had a niece and a nephew. *Goodness,* thought Sally, *I might be all right if we get passed babyhood but carrying a small infant up and down the stairs. Goodness, the laundry room is on the ground floor, and I'll be spending a lot of time there, can I do it?*

Then she remembered that, she had done more than one thing at once, and was considered a multitasking marvel (At least by her colleagues at Ormsbury), so she could not let them down. Others had done it. Else there would be no human race. If Ralph could help where he could, she would manage. Then she thought of actually giving birth, and going to ante-natal classes, and the pain that the birth would entail. But everybody said it was something you forgot afterwards, otherwise no one would have more than one child, so she would not think about that just yet. *Goodness, what on earth have I got myself into?* she thought and to ease her mind she turned towards the sleeping Ralph and put her arms around him. He grunted at that, and snuggled next to him she dozed off.

They both woke early, and together, they went into to the bathroom and Ralph sat on the bathroom stool while he waited for Sally to perform. Together they looked for the result to show, and it was positive. Ralph put his arms around Sally and held her tight, they had talked about this, and now it had happened.

"How do you feel?" he asked.

"A bit shattered," she said. "I have spent all night wondering about it. How do you feel?"

"As though I have just got to the top of the rock face, and I'm looking down on the world. This is absolutely fantastic. We'll get through this together." This was the answer to Sally's earlier worry.

"Phew!" she said. "I was a bit worried about how you would take the news."

"It's going to make a big change in our lives," Ralph said. "But I'll help in any way I can, you should know that."

"Yes, I do, love. I just had one of my worry spells."

"You are a chump. Come on let's have breakfast."

"They went down to the kitchen and together prepared the meal." While they were eating Sally told Ralph about her other thoughts.

"I wasn't feeling 100% before, and I am definitely going to drop out of *Calamity Jane* now," she said. "Also, it came to me today," she continued, "that I have really enjoyed doing the research on this project and want to carry on. So until I found out about the change in our circumstances (Bit pompous, ain't I?), I thought I would go for a higher degree. What do you think?"

"I think that's a great idea," was Ralph's immediate response. "And you can be pregnant and do one as well. Why not go and talk to the department in the morning?"

"Which department would that be?"

"I think, knowing you, it will be history but there might be a bit of Anglo-Saxon in there somewhere," he grinned at her.

"I think medieval, don't you?" said Sally with a smile. "Now then, how is ASS going?"

144

"I have submitted my ideas for the Literature segment of the programme. That has been agreed. Unfortunately, some of the others haven't got around to finalising their submissions so it is all going to take some time. I have had a call from Marsha, to see how we are getting on, as she seems to think her reputation is at stake over it. But now it is in the hands of the Jorvik, it is surely up to us?"

"I just think that she likes to keep her eye on you," said Sally. "But this latest news might knock her sideways!"

"You mean the infant?" asked Ralph. "She is not going to be able to compete with that."

"So, we are all good," asked Sally.

"Absolutely bloody fantastic," replied Ralph.

Chapter 42

The University Term had started and the time drifted on. Sally began going back to Gisburn and picked up her old routine with the wills. She assisted Arthur Cliff writing the explanatory booklet which would go with the exhibition of the documents. She also wrote an article for the Richard III's Society 'Ricardian' magazine, which she was going to submit as soon as the news was released. In the meantime, she grew into her pregnancy.

The History Faculty had been very accommodating and had offered a place in their Ph.D. programme beginning in the autumn. They had taken her situation into consideration and decided that as it was to be a thesis, rather than a lecture-based degree she could do it over a three-year period. As she had already done so much work on the objects for the display, it was inevitable that her thesis was going to be on a companion subject, and she began gathering the background information that would need. The exhibition was scheduled to take place just before the beginning of the Summer Term and the invitations to the great and the good of the locality had gone out. One of those was to the Chancellor of St James's University, which reminded Marsha that she had, as yet not had her coffee morning with Sally.

Therefore, it was during the middle of March that Sally received a phone call inviting her to coffee in the Assembly Rooms in Blake Street. At 11 am, Marsha sailed into the Assembly Rooms to find Sally already seated. Marsha, as usual, was elegant and sophisticated, while Sally, who rose to greet her was wearing the loosest clothes she could find to hide her burgeoning bump. Marsha immediately recognised the camouflage for what it was, and, while she had heard rumours, was disconcerted to find that they were true.

They sat down at the table and a hovering waiter took their order. While they waited for their order to arrive, they exchanged pleasantries and, after Sally's hot chocolate and Marsha's flat white arrived, they got down to business.

"I was right," Marsha said. "Ralph looks so much happier now that he is going to be a media star."

"I'm sorry," said Sally. "I think that you are wrong there."

"But the producer says that the camera loves him and that he can go far."

"That's as maybe. But it only works if he wants it."

"How do you mean?"

"He doesn't want to be a star, he never did. That's where you made your mistake."

"I beg your pardon," said Marsha.

"Ralph told me that while you were together, you were constantly pushing him this way and that. To be what you wanted him to be."

"What's wrong with that? Some men need a strong woman behind them in order to get on." Marsha had strong ideas about men.

"That's true but Ralph isn't one of them."

"Go on."

"He is a bit geeky, nerdy even but he knows what he wants. Maybe he was a bit of a late developer but he got there in the end."

"Where? The back of beyond?" said Marsha.

"Teaching Anglo-Saxon Literature at Jorvik University?" Sally was getting cross.

"That's not very ambitious."

"No but that's what he wants to do. He is only doing the TV programmes to further that. If the department closes, he will lose his job and have to start again."

There was a pause and Marsha said, "You said you saw him first."

"When did I say that?" asked Sally.

"At the dinner party."

"You remember that? Well, it's true, I did."

"When was that?"

"It was at Leeds University. I was a Library Assistant in the Brotherton, when he was an undergraduate." Sally laughed. "He spent the whole of his final term asking me to go to the Union Bar for a drink. It was a nasty smoky place in those days, and I refused each time. He used to squirm his way around the catalogues when I was looking something up, and the first thing I saw was his lanky, greasy hair coming around the corner. He didn't stand up straight in order to hide his height in those days. His hair hid his face. I'm not sure I actually ever saw it properly."

"How did you meet up again?"

"It was a long time afterwards when he went to West Lancs U, on a two-year contract. By then, you had met him when he did his Ph.D. When we met again, he had cleaned and smartened up and needed my help. Together we solved the mystery which had been bugging him. It was only later that he found a photograph taken at his graduation, when he and his mates had dragged me out of the Brotherton to be in the picture, that we recognised one another."

"Where did I go wrong?" asked Marsha.

"As far as I can tell, from what he has said. It was the pushing him to go in directions that he did not want to go in. What he needs in encouragement to get where he wants to be," said Sally the faithful wife.

"And you give him that?"

"Well, he gives it to me too."

"But he is going to be a celebrity."

"No, he's not. He is only doing the programme on literature. The others are doing their bit. It's going to be a departmental effort, with a neutral presenter brining it all together."

"So, he is happy then?" Marsha was a bit put out. "Where do you fit in?"

"As you know, I am a Librarian, and what I enjoy most is find information for the readers. My current reader is Ralph. So, I support him and at the moment, he is supporting me. I've been accepted for a PhD."

Then Marsha decided it was time to notice the bump. "You're expecting?" she said.

"Yes, that is another reason he is happy."

"I can't compete with that," said Marsha. "When is it due?"

"In about six months."

"So, I don't suppose you would like a job at St James?"

"Not at the moment, thank you. I'm rather busy. A year ago, I would probably have jumped at the chance but now all has changed."

"Don't give up your own ambitions." Marsha had become the head mistress now.

"I haven't and Ralph is supporting me. I want to do research, that is why I'm doing the Ph.D."

"So, there is nothing for me here?" said Marsha rather sadly. "How could I get it so wrong? I've always prided myself on being a good judge of character, so where did I go wrong with Ralph? I thought he had ambition. He was always talking about what he wanted to do. I thought he wanted what I wanted but he didn't."

"He did have ambition but to go in a completely different direction to that which you were offering."

Marsha picked up the bill. "Perhaps we'll bump into each other again. Good luck," she said and left leaving Sally alone at the table.

"I think we've seen the last of Marsha," she told Ralph when she got home.

Chapter 43

At the end of April, which was the beginning of the Summer Term, the letter and its pouch and the receipt together with the surrounding authentication were ready to reveal to the waiting world. Except, of course, as yet the world did not know about them and so were totally unprepared for the revelation.

On Monday, 29th April, a press conference was organised in York at the Gisburn Archive, of Jorvik University. The national and local press were invited, and at 10 am the announcement was made. On the walls were photographic blown-up images of the two documents, as well as photographs of the pouch showing the inscription which had kept it safe for more than 400 years. Dr Stanley Fisher was in charge but included in his team were Sally Armstrong and Arthur Cliff.

"Ladies and Gentlemen," began Dr Fisher, "on the walls behind me, you can see images of the documents and the pouch which were given to the Gisburn Archive. Over the last few weeks, they have been rigorously tested and their provenance has been investigated and we are now able to announce that the letter that you see behind me, was written sometime after 1487 by Richard of Shrewsbury, also Duke of York, and tells of the death of his brother King Edward V, and his own escape to Burgundy, with aide provided by his uncle, King Richard III. From Burgundy, he tells of his adventures on the continent, and his decision to seek a quiet, private life, and not to meddle in the politics of England. This information, which is now confirmed as authentic, at last, lays to rest, one of the last calumnies against Richard III. This, together with the discovery of the late king's remains in Leicester, has enabled the academic world to reassess the events of the late king's reign, and to remove some of the lies and deceits, which have clouded our view of his reign. An exhibition of the items is being made available and will be on view to the general public from Thursday, 2nd May. A formal opening is being held here in the university on the evening of 1 May. Are there any questions?"

The room erupted. A handout was available of Dr Fisher's speech which had included the wording of the letter, and that on the pouch, and the receipt. As it was passed around several papers floated over the heads of those seated, while others fell to the floor, in the mad rush to get a better look at the photographs. Stanley Fisher, Sally and Arthur were rather lost in the crush and Ralph was concerned for the safety of his heavily pregnant wife. He managed to disentangle her from the throng and sat her on a chair at the side of the room where soon a small gathering of reporters gathered to find out both who she was, and what part she had played in the discovery. She explained as best she could to the questions being fired at her, as did Stanley and Arthur who had also become separated, and isolated in different corners of the room. Eventually, the crowd disappeared as the reporters began looking for a quiet corner of their own to make their initial reports to their newspapers over their mobile phones.

Over the next two days, reports appeared in the press and Sally and Ralph bought copies of all the papers, to see how the revelation was reported. Most were very interested but gave only limited information. Dr Fisher rang to say that the opening exhibition was now over-subscribed and would be a big success. Several of the newspapers got hold of tame historians, who reported more fully on the significance of the discovery, which repeated most of the arguments which Sally had used in her discussions with Ralph. Only one report was critical. In this, the anonymous historian claimed that the documents were fakes and that the exhibition was a hoax and warned everybody not to have anything to do with it. By going online, Sally was able to identify this anonymous writer, as a die-hard historian who subscribed to the "There is nothing good that can be said about Richard III" school of thought. When Sally read that, she said, "Do you know, love? I think that there is a society somewhere, of people who will never change their minds about their pet subject, no matter how much proof to the contrary you can put in front of them."

"You mean like the Flat Earth Society?" replied Ralph.

"Or those people who think that the Americans never landed on the moon?"

"Or conspiracy theorists in general? What about the people that are convinced that Battle of Brunanburh was at Bromborough? Though I don't think there is a society about that." The Anglo-Saxon scholar in Ralph, was not going to let this flight of fancy go without mentioning the opponents of his pet theory.

"Yes. If there is such a society, do you think that they will have nice quiet meetings putting their views forward, or do you think they will all be challenging one another, with the meetings ending in a riot? Do you think that they would naturally disbelieve anything that came out of the North of England on principle?"

"Now that is getting divisive. I think we had better leave this fancy alone before we start a civil war."

"Anyway, my love, the one thing that has been settled is, that you can never again wind me up by telling me that Richard III murdered the Princes in the Tower." Sally grinned.

"Damn," said Ralph very forcefully, "that was often the one bit of enjoyment that I got in a dull week."

And they both laughed.

Chapter 44

Wednesday, May 1st, marked the date of the release of the discovery and the consequent publicity. The press conference on 29th April had generated a great deal of interest, as had the subsequence press reports. As it was a significant landmark in the rehabilitation of King Richard III, the invitations had gone out to the great and the good. There were a limited number of tickets for members of the public for a fee, and these had been taken up quickly. There was a great deal of interest.

A report, largely based on the one Sally had written for Dr Fisher, was produced and concerned the history of the pouch, the letter and the receipt. Arthur Cliff had written a history of Richard of Shrewsbury/York and the importance of the information that had been discovered. He was well versed about the 3rd Baron Conyers who had made the donation to Crayke but Sally had provided the details about Sir John Conyers, who was the original recipient of the letter. It was a collaborative effort, and copies were to be given to all the invited guests and it was also on sale to the public.

The Truth about the 'Princes in the Tower'

King Edward IV died unexpectedly on 9th April 1483 and his eldest son Edward, was proclaimed king on 11 April. However, the new king Edward aged 12 was at his castle home at Ludlow in Shropshire, and the news of his father's death did not reach him until 14 April. He did not leave Ludlow until 24th April, when an armed force lead by Earl Rivers and Sir Thomas Vaughan, arrived to escort the new king to London. Meanwhile, the late king was buried in his newly built, St George's Chapel in Windsor Castle on 20th April. He had attempted to smooth the path of his successor but by dying suddenly, his heir was far away, and his brother Richard Duke of Gloucester was also far away on his Middleham estates in Yorkshire. He also received the news of his brother's death on about 14th April.

Faction ensued with the Queen's Woodville family, seeking to overturn the late King's will, which made his brother Richard the sole protector and guardian of the new king, during his minority. The Queen wished to hasten the coronation of her son to enable him to rule in his own right. A date was set of the 4th May for the coronation. This was not well received by the nobility as they feared the rule of a juvenile who could be controlled by others. Richard, Duke of Gloucester having heard of his brother's death on about 14th April had left Middleham for York on about 20th April. He left York on 23rd April after taking an oath of fealty to his nephew, the new king.

On 29th April, the King's procession from Ludlow, and the Duke of Gloucester's from York, met at Stony Stratford, and the Dukes of Buckingham and Gloucester arrested Rivers, Grey and Vaughan and assured the King of their loyalty to him. When the news of the arrests reached London, the Queen fled with her children to sanctuary in Westminster Abbey. The news of Gloucester's coming was generally greeted with pleasure by the people of London. On 4th May, the king and both Dukes arrived in London. Following this, a council was held at which it was decided to lodge the King in the Tower of London, until his coronation, where he had arrived by 19th May. On 16th June, he was joined by his brother Richard Duke of York. They are reputed to have never left it again. On 22nd June, sermons alleging the bastardy of the sons of Edward IV were given, together with the evidence of Edward IV's pre-contract with Lady Eleanor Butler, who had not died until after Edward's secret marriage with Elizabeth Woodville, proved that they were illegitimate and that Edward should not rule. At this point, Gloucester became the monarch. His coronation was held on 6th July.

The young boys in the Tower were regularly attended by doctors until sometime in August, they were seen no more. At this point, rumour takes over.

The document and the pouch, which has been generously donated to the Gisburn Archive and whose identity has been carefully authenticated prove beyond doubt that Richard III did not murder the princes in the Tower. We know from Richard of York's letter what happened next. Edward the elder boy died at the Tower and was buried privily at Windsor by Sir James Tyrell who then transported the younger boy to his home at Gipping where his mother, Elizabeth, visited him before he was sent across the sea to Burgundy.

The letter appears to have been written at some point in the late 1480s. It is undated but shows that Richard of York, also known as Richard of Shrewsbury, lived long after his uncle died. He also states that, he had no intention of making himself known to the world and that he gave up any claim to the throne. That claim, first made by his grandfather, Richard Duke of York, had brought nothing but tragedy to the family.

This new knowledge, that Richard III did not murder either of the boys while they were in the Tower, has finally scotched the calumny of murder, as has speculation that any one of a number of other people, including Margaret Beaufort and Henry VII were responsible for the deaths.

However, this does not answer any of the other questions which arise from these events.

Why were there pretenders in the shape of Lambert Simnel in 1487 and Perkin Warbeck in 1495–7?

Why did Henry VII not proclaim the death of the boys early in his reign? He accused Richard III of the death of innocents but was not specific?

Why did he fear a last gasp outpouring of support for the house of York, long after he was safely on the throne? He continued to execute anyone who had a claim, as did his son Henry VIII.

And why did Sir James Tyrell confess to killing the boys in 1502?

Was Perkin Warbeck really Richard Duke of York? Is so why did he confess he was to son of a barge owner from Tournai.

One interesting aspect of the affair is why did Richard of York write in this way to Sir John Conyers? Sir John Conyers, had in the past, been a Lancastrian supporter at the time of Henry VI, and had appeared as Robin of Redesdale at the time of the Yorkshire Rebellion of 1469, when the Earl of Warwick attempted to overthrow Edward IV. In March 1470, he had again supported the Lincolnshire Rebellion of the Nevilles'. It was only after the return of Edward from Flanders and the appointment of Richard, Duke of Gloucester to the former Neville estates of Middleham, that he changed his allegiance to the Yorkist cause. Perhaps his close working relationship with Gloucester, which had begun with Gloucester's visit to Hornby in 1470, was what had changed his mind. Thus, it was that in response to an enquiry as to the health of the last of the Plantagenets, that Richard of York, felt able to tell his story. We will never know.

It is said that "Truth is the daughter of time." Perhaps if we live long enough, we will all find out the truth.

Arthur Cliff and S. A. Armstrong.

The exhibition, by the Gisburn Archive, had been prepared in the university's main lecture theatre. Among the great and the good who gathered there were the Mayor of York, the Lord Lieutenant of the County, The Archbishop of York, The Dean of the Cathedral, the Chancellor of Jorvik University and members of the Senate, and Marsha Hamilton as Chancellor of St James's University.

Ralph had not seen Marsha to speak to since the dinner party the previous summer but she had espied him on the University campus during one of her visits to the Jorvik and had noticed the change in his demeanour. He had however, had a report of the coffee morning from Sally. For once, Ralph was Sally's plus one, rather than the other way around. He dutifully stood behind her shoulder during the evening, until after the speeches. It was while the buffet was being taken that Marsha finally managed to edge him away from the throng.

"I understand congratulations are in order," she opened.

"Yes, thank you. I am very proud of Sally's contribution to the evening," was his response.

"Don't be funny. You know what I mean," she said.

Ralph laughed. Marsha realised she had never heard him laugh. He was happy.

"You're really happy, aren't you?"

He nodded.

"I really was wrong, trying to fit you into my idea of the future, as I have been told. Wasn't I?"

"No, you just tried to push me in a direction that I did not want to go."

"You've really found your niche?" she asked. She knew from Sally that that was the case but found it surprising.

"I sure have," he said. "No hard feelings?"

"No," Marsha said. "It's all in the past now. I understand that Sally has found her niche as well."

"Yes," was his reply. "We've been very fortunate. Sally's going for a Ph.D. as she wants to do research. I think, deep down, that is what she has always wanted to do. She has a knack of going at things backwards. This project" – he indicated the exhibition – "has been a good start for her."

"Not only that, there's a family on the way."

"Things can't get any better." He smiled.

156

"Good luck." And Marsha drifted away. As she went, Ralph followed her and said, "Actually, there is someone over there who is dying to meet you." Taking her arm, he led Marsha towards Arthur Cliff and his wife, who were talking to the Archbishop. Arthur was explaining to the Archbishop, who had no idea of the breadth of Yorkshire history, or of the depth of feeling that the discovery had provoked. As he was not a Yorkshireman, he found it a little overwhelming, and as Marsha and Ralph approached, he managed to disentangle himself from Arthur and passed on to the Mayor.

"Mr and Mrs Cliff," said Ralph, as he caught up with them. "I should like to introduce you to Dr Marsha Hamilton, Chancellor of St James's University." Then to Marsha he said, "Mr Cliff is a big fan of yours."

He left them talking and went to find Sally who was sitting in the lecture theatre gathering her breath. She had not had to make any speeches but her contribution had been pointed out and several of the visitors and found her and questioned her about what she had done. She had also spent some time introducing Miss Atherton to Mrs Osborne and showing them the exhibits, and how they fitted together. Now she was just glad to sit and rest her legs.

As the evening wore on, people began to drift away and eventually, Sally and Ralph could leave.

As they left, they could see that Arthur and his wife were deep in conversation with Marsha.

"Do you think I still need to organise that dinner party for them?" Sally asked.

"I'll have a word with Arthur," Ralph replied. "But at the rate they are going, I don't think you'll have to."

"That's a relief. I don't think I could stand it just now."

Later that evening when they were safely back at home, Sally hugged Ralph.

"I love you," she said. "Thank you for your support, my love. I couldn't have done that without you. Do you know? I can't believe that just was it only 18 months ago that I was crashing pans and getting depressed and look at me now."

"I remember the pans," said Ralph. "I thought that I was going to get them on my head."

"And now a future," said Sally. "Not what I set out for but a baby, a degree, and the possibility of a career which I can control. Oh! Darling, thank you." She hugged him again and he held her close.

"Yes love, it's going to be great," he murmured into her hair.

Epilogue

Some months later and strange noises were coming from the Armstrong residence.

"Hwast! We Gardena in geardagumþeodycyninga, þrymgefrunon, *(Hear me! We've heard of Danish heroes, Ancient kings and the glory they cut),"* crooned Ralph to the dozing child nestled in his arms, "hu ðaaeþelingas Ellen fremedon! *(For themselves swinging mighty swords!)."* His sonorous voice lent the Anglo-Saxon epic a particular resonance as he gently used the one talent he felt he had in trying to get his son to sleep.

"You are going to spoil the Scrap," said Sally from the kitchen. "He's not going to take any notice of me when I sing him a lullaby after that, you know."

"Well, you know I can't sing like you, I just growl. I decided tonight on the way home, that I was going to give my son the best start in life, by giving him good examples to follow."

"You know I love the sound of your voice declaiming Beowulf but aren't you going to give the poor scrap a complex or something? He's going to be the only boy in his nursery class who is more familiar with Anglo-Saxon than English."

"I've decided that I am going to start as I mean to go on, besides calling him Scrap is not going to do his confidence any good. I mean 'What is your name, son?', 'Scrap, sir!' He's not going to get into Eton with a name like that."

"He's not going to Eton anyway or at least if he does it will be over my dead body. But going back to Beowulf, do you think you could at least translate as you go on?"

"I might consider it for a small fee," he said as Sally came through from the kitchen. She bent over and gave him a big kiss.

"Is that small enough?" she asked.

"Just about right. Now then, where was I? O yes, *'How Shild made slaves of soldiers from every land he'd beaten into terror; he'd travelled into Denmark*

158

alone, an abandoned child, but changed his own fate.' That's the bit I think, will do him the most good. Knowing that you can change your own fate. We did."

"You have a point there, but I still think Beowulf is a bit heavy going for a three-week old."

"You may be right but if I try to stop myself going all Anglo-Saxon, will you try to find a name for him? We will have to register him soon. 'Scrap' does not inspire confidence."

"I just look at him and think, you poor scrap of humanity and I don't get passed that. But you are right. I have tried other names, and we've talked about it till the cows come home, but nothing seems to suit him. Besides why have you given me the job?"

"You didn't like any of the names I came up with."

"You only came up with Anglo-Saxon ones. If we stick with the period, it's going to be Harold or Edward or William of Henry. I like Richard but I'm afraid he'll be called Dick, and I don't like that. We want a name that can't be shortened," Sally announced as she went back to look at the dinner.

"I rather like Anglo-Saxon and Norse names," Ralph muttered to his son. "I want you to have ambition, to be fearless, unlike your daft dad, and go on Emley Moor and find the dragon that I never managed to find."

A couple of days later, while Ralph, who was just starting his fourth year at Jorvik University, was cycling home from the campus he had his brilliant idea. It was while he made these journeys, and negotiated York's traffic, that he thought about his son and his ambitions for him.

Their son had been born in York, thus making him a Yorkshireman, for which they were both eternally grateful. As yet the child had no name. Sally called him Scrap but Ralph had a different name for him each time he came home and tried each in turn, working on the assumption that one would eventually suit, and looking into his tiny eyes he would know that that was who his child was. This was the only subject that did not agree on. Both were willing to make compromises but a name was very important to both of them. All through Sally's pregnancy they had discussed names, but not knowing the sex of the child, meant that the final decision could not be made until after his arrival. On looking into the baby's eyes, they knew that their choices were all wrong. Soon they would have to make a decision time was running out. Whatever name went on the birth certificate would have to be the one.

Time was marching on, a decision would soon have to be made, and his son's birth registered. He had stopped at the lights at the end of his road when he had his brainwave. Turning into the home straight, he pushed the cycle into the garage and went into the kitchen. No Sally. He went through to the front room to find Sally with Scrap in her arms feeding him. She looked the picture of maternal perfection.

He gave her a kiss.

"I've just had a brainwave," he said. "Why don't we call him Gawain? I know it was one of the names we discounted but Gawain was a hero, so it fits the hero criteria, and it could be corrupted to Wayne, and would not make him stand out. What do you think?"

"I think it's a terrible idea," said Sally smiling at him. "Think of the ribbing he will get at school. But why don't we call him something simple, like John, shortened to Jon, with Gawain as a middle name. Then, when he begins to write all those important works of literature or science or whatever he could call himself J. Gawain Armstrong if he wants to?"

"I rather like that," said Ralph, he rolled the name on his tongue. "My son, the well-known whatever J. Gawain Armstrong. I like it."

"Actually, 'John' was just a suggestion but if you like it, I'll go along with it, the poor darling needs a name."

"Right, that's settled. What's for tea?"

Historical Note

This novel is a work of fiction. The letter from Richard of York does not exist. However, certain historical characters did exist including Sir John Conyers (Died 1490) and his descendants including Sir Christopher Conyers (Died 1538). William Allanson of York leased the castle in 1648 and it was his son Charles who restored the castle after the Civil War before it was returned to the Diocese of Durham. The ancestors of Alice Atherton are figments of my imagination.

To date, no document or letter has been found to confirm the fate of the Princes in the Tower, and the legend of Richard III's involvement will no doubt continue. Someday such a document will be found and ultimately the truth will be known.